THE MANY LIVES OF GEORGIE WELLS

IVY MYSTERY SERIES - BOOK 4

MICHELLE FILES

PUBLISHED BY BOOKLOVERS PUBLISHING

INTRODUCTION

It's never too late to die and try again.

Georgie Wells dies at 18. The first time she relives her life, she comes back at 13 years old, and has a mystery to solve: She's living with a family she has never met.

Over several lifetimes, Georgie struggles in a desperate race through time to solve the mystery, and her own death, looking over her shoulder at every turn.

Teens and adults alike will love this time travel thriller.

Get your copy of this gripping time travel series. This is the fourth book in the Ivy Mystery Series.

The Many Lives of Ivy Wells – Book 1
The Many Lives of Sam Wells – Book 2
The Many Lives of Jack Wells – Book 3
The Many Lives of Georgie Wells – Book 4

Novels by Michelle Files:

TYLER MYSTERY SERIES:
Girl Lost
A Reckless Life

WILDFLOWER MYSTERY SERIES:
Secrets of Wildflower Island
Desperation on Wildflower Island
Storm on Wildflower Island
Thorns on Wildflower Island

IVY MYSTERY SERIES:
The Many Lives of Ivy Wells
The Many Lives of Sam Wells
The Many Lives of Jack Wells
The Many Lives of Georgie Wells

STONE MOUNTAIN FAMILY SAGA:
Winters Legend on Stone Mountain
A Dangerous Game on Stone Mountain
Deceit on Stone Mountain

For information on any of Michelle's books:
www.MichelleFiles.com

PART 1

CHAPTER 1

The first time I died, I was completely unprepared. Now... nothing surprises me at all.

Before I even opened my eyes that morning, I could feel the aches and pains in my body. I felt bruised from head to toe, my mind searching for answers to the pain. But in the fogginess of my early morning brain, I couldn't remember anything. A sudden chill caused my entire body to shiver. Why was it so cold?

I reached around behind me for my blankets, figuring I had kicked them off in the middle of the night. All I felt was debris and hard ground next to me. I jerked my hand toward me when something sharp pierced my palm. My eyes flew open.

It was almost pitch black. No familiar night-light on the wall of my bedroom. Though I was an adult, I always kept a night-light in my room. The night terrified me.

I was definitely not in my room. Through the trees above me, I could see a sliver of a moon. The crescent moon. A symbol of surrender, rest, recuperation. I felt none of those things. Only cold, afraid, and confused.

I was in the forest somewhere and had no idea how I had gotten there. Pushing myself up into a seated position, I scanned as far as I could see. It wasn't far. The crescent moon only put off a dull glow in the dense forest.

Searching my memory, I had no idea how I had arrived where I was. And in the state I was. Wait...I thought for a moment...something was just on the edge, trying to work its way in. A flash in my mind. No words, just pictures. My mother. Then a woman I didn't recognize. But who could be sure? She was there, then gone in a flash. A girl I didn't know. Then I saw my sister and brother, Harper and Jack.

What was happening? Why was I seeing my family, and others that I didn't know? And why was I in the forest, in the middle of the night? Had I been sleepwalking?

The clothing I was wearing felt hard and crusty. As my hand touched my blouse, my mind searched for answers. What was that on my blouse? Was that mud? It couldn't be...blood. Could it? The answer to that question was impossible to find in the little bit of illumination that was around me.

I needed to get out of there. Wherever that was.

I stood, wincing in pain as I did. Everything hurt. Everything. But I couldn't stay in the forest in the middle of the night. I needed to get home. I didn't even know if I was in Red Lake and I had no idea which direction to walk in. But I got up anyway and begin walking. I headed toward the moon. At least it was something I could keep my eye on, and keep me from walking around in circles in the forest. The only result from that would be freezing to death.

I walked for hours, wincing in pain each time I stepped on a rock or pine cone. My bare feet began to bleed. Why in the world was I barefoot? I jumped at every little sound in the dense forest. Every critter that scurried. Every flapping of a wing overhead. It was all so intensified by the darkness and the eeriness of my surroundings.

I didn't know why, but I couldn't stop. I had to keep moving. Something else jumped into my mind. I didn't know what to make of of it. But I knew that I couldn't let him find me.

Who? Searching my memories, I couldn't find the answer to that question. It was there, though. I was right on the tip of it. But, no, whoever it was that I feared, he wasn't showing himself to me. Not yet anyway.

I held my arms and shivered as I made my way out. At least I thought I was heading out. Truth is that I really had no clear idea where I was heading. Or why.

In the deep, dark, blackness of the forest, I had to watch every step I took. But I couldn't see three feet in front of me. I prayed that I wouldn't stumble onto a family of mountain lions, or even bears. The thought made me tremble. As I continued listening for signs of wildlife...a guttural growl, a roar, or even a yip of a coyote, it happened. I never saw it in front of me.

A hole in the ground. With no time to contemplate what that meant for me, down I went.

And no, not just a quick tumble into a shallow hole in the ground, causing a few scuffs, or even a fractured arm. It was deep. Really deep. It was almost as if I was in suspended animation as I descended at a rapid pace. In my mind, I saw myself slamming into jagged rocks, my neck snapping upon impact.

That didn't happen.

I felt the shocking chill of ice cold water, causing me to gasp. It wasn't deep though. Just deep enough to slow me down, before I hit the bottom. And I hit it hard. It felt almost as if my back broke as the wind was knocked from my lungs. I needed to get to the surface. And fast. I had no reserves of air left to tide me over for a few seconds while I got my bearings. I already had that desperate feeling of needing to take a deep breath to refill my lungs once again.

Resisting the urge to gulp in air, which I knew would be disastrous at the bottom of that murky hole, my arms flailed, desperately seeking the surface. My feet actually hit the bottom just as my head made it above the water. I drew in the night air as fast as my lungs would allow. It took at least a full minute of gasping breaths before I felt some semblance of normal breathing. My head was swimming with stars, while I was fighting an impending blackout.

I stood. The water was only about waist deep. For the first time, I tried to look around, but there was almost no light so far beneath the surface of the earth. How far down was I actually? I couldn't tell. Looking up, I could see the tops of some trees, but from where I stood, I had no way of telling how far they were.

This couldn't be the sinkhole, could it? The one that was deep in the forest? Was I that far in? I was familiar with the sinkhole, of course. Every teenager in the area had hung out there at one time or another. I was no different.

The sinkhole had been ordered off limits. The city had even put fencing around it. Many times. Along with warning signs. The problem was that it was gradually getting wider and wider. The fencing always caved in eventually.

If that's where I was, then it wasn't currently blocked off, which didn't surprise me. But how did I survive a fall in? Others hadn't been so lucky over the years.

Something brushed my leg. "What the…" Envisioning the bones of one of those unfortunate souls who had gone in before me, I wanted no more of that sinkhole, or whatever kind of hole I had found myself in.

"I really need to get out of here." Yes, I was prone to talking to myself. It's what kept me sane.

My body shivered, involuntarily, and I wrapped my arms in front to help stave off the cold. It wasn't working. I needed to act quickly.

"Oh, Georgie, what have you gotten yourself into?" I asked out loud. No response.

Though I really couldn't see anything, I instinctively knew that going up was out of the question. That was not going to happen.

"There has to be another way out. The water is going somewhere." Speaking more in a whisper made me feel safer somehow.

I stuck my hands out in front of me, in the dark, trying to find a wall. I noticed that the sand was soft beneath my bare feet. Three steps forward, and I felt a wall. It was not hard stone, like I expected. It was dirt. Mud actually. I could pull handfuls of it out of the wall.

"Stop. You are going to pull the entire wall of mud down on top of you, Dummy."

Following carefully along the wall, a few minutes later I came upon a tunnel. My eyes were beginning to adjust to the darkness, and I could just make out where the tunnel went through from where I was standing, the water flowing freely through it.

"Okay, now we're talking. This has to lead somewhere."

A shiver ran up my spine. It wouldn't be long before hypothermia set in. I needed to get moving.

The tunnel was lower than my height, by about a foot, so I bent over and continued along. My head wasn't far above the water. If the elevation of the bottom changed, I might have a problem.

Moving slowly, I wasn't making a lot of progress, that was obvious. But I was fearful of taking a wrong step and finding myself in an even worse predicament than I was already in.

It was getting darker and darker, the further I moved into the tunnel. That was a bad sign. That told me that there was no light, no opening ahead.

Boom. I ran smack into a wall. This one was not soft mud,

like what I had found in the hole behind me. This wall was hard rock. It had come upon me so quickly that I didn't even realize that it was there. My nose exploded in pain, and though I couldn't see it, I could feel the warm blood gushing down the front of my face. The metallic taste moistened my lips.

"Dammit! A broken nose is all I need right now!" I yelled to the walls of my watery prison.

Reaching into the ice cold water I was standing in, I did what I could to clean away the blood. I had to do my best, as I couldn't see much at all. My legs and torso were turning numb from the cold as I waited for my nose to stop bleeding.

Reaching up to the wall in front of me, I realized that it was not solid. It was full of hard rocks, but they were mixed in with dirt and mud. Pulling at one of them, I was able to remove it from the wall. Then another, and another. But really, where was that going to get me? I couldn't possibly dig through who knows how many feet, or miles maybe, of wall.

"No, this isn't going to work. I need to find another way."

Just as I turned to head back down that tunnel, toward the way I had come from, I felt a low rumbling under my feet. I didn't realize what was going on at first, but it didn't take long for that to change. Within only seconds, the walls started to rumble around me, ever increasing in volume and intensity. My heart began to race as I looked around desperately for some sort of escape. When some of the rocks began to shake loose and fall from the walls, and splash with a thunk around my feet, panic set in.

I turned toward where I thought I had come from, but I had gotten turned around and I really didn't know where I was. It was still so dark in there. Through the loud roar that was surrounding me by that point, I was still able to manage to reach out and find a wall. Rocks were tumbling all around me. When one hit me in the shoulder, I cried out in pain, positive that it may have broken my arm. Or at the very least, torn a good size gash in it.

As more and more rocks tumbled down around me, I kept getting hit. There was no way to avoid them. I began to run down the length of the tunnel, though I had no idea where I was heading. The whole earth seem to be coming down around me. My heart was racing. My breathing became labored. When I stumbled over a boulder in the water, I went face down and hit the bottom. I struggled to get up, rocks still pummeling me.

About the time I found the spot where I had fallen down into the hole, I looked up and could see the walls crashing down all around me. I cried out with a desperation I had never known before. I was about to die. I knew that. And I knew there was not a damn thing I could do about it.

My final thoughts were of my family. My mother, Ivy. My sister, Harper, and my brother, Jack. I knew they would be devastated without me. They would never know what happened to me. No one would ever find my body buried under 20 or 30 feet of dirt and mud and rocks. My broken body would forever remain hidden from those that loved me.

And what about my other family? Will they mourn me? Yes, they will. No time to think about it all. My time had come.

I cried out as a small boulder bore down on me. When it slammed into my head, it exploded with pain. The freezing water and my numb legs were forgotten. My fear no longer existed.

Before I even had a chance to contemplate what had just occurred, I sunk below the surface of the water and everything went black.

CHAPTER 2

"Georgie...Georgie? Are you all right?" It was a woman's voice, that I didn't recognize.

Laughter erupted all around me. Before I was truly aware of it, it seemed to float above my head and through the ceiling.

Looking down, I realized I was lying face down on a hard tile floor. I grabbed the nearest piece of furniture and pulled myself to a seated position in some sort of desk.

"Georgie...hello?"

Someone jabbed me in the back just below my right shoulder, jolting me back into reality. Turning to confront the jabber, I saw a fresh faced boy, with shaggy hair, no more than 12 or 13 years old. He grinned at me and I furrowed my brows in his direction.

"Wake up, dummy. The teacher is trying to get your attention." The boy snickered as he spoke, pointing toward the front of the room.

Who me? I never actually said that to him. That's when I turned around in my seat and realized there were probably 20 or 30 additional fresh faced teens sitting at desks all around me.

Every single one of those eyeballs was pointing in my direction. I felt the heat rise from my chest all the way to my forehead.

Shivering, I wrapped my arms around in front of me. My feet ached and I looked down at them, expecting to find them bruised and bloody. Instead, I found that I was adorned with pink tennis shoes. I stared at my feet much longer than I probably should have. I could still feel everyone watching me.

"What?...Where am I?" Those words I actually did say out loud, and they were met with a roar of laughter from all the students around me.

"Georgie, are you all right?" It was the woman's voice again.

I turned toward her. It was obviously the teacher in the classroom I was sitting in. But I didn't understand what was going on. Why was I sitting in a classroom full of pre-teens?

"Um, yeah." I looked around again at all of the curious faces watching me intently. "I don't...I don't feel very well. I need to go."

Standing up, I turned to leave.

"Georgie, where do you think you're going?" the teacher asked me.

"I...I don't belong here. This is some sort of mistake. I just need to go."

Not waiting for a response, I turned and bolted for the door. There was nothing but silence behind me. Probably stunned silence at my behavior. I didn't care at that moment. There was nothing more in the world I needed right then but to get out of that room.

Finding myself in the hallway of the school, I turned left and then right, scanning the empty hallways. Though I saw no one, I knew exactly where I was. A middle school. Based on the ages of the kids, I assumed it was a middle school anyway. It was definitely some sort of school. But why was I in a school? I was 18 years old and hadn't been in middle school in years. Why in the world would I find myself sitting in the middle of a class-room full of young teens?

It was a good question, and it was one that I had no idea how to answer. Not hesitating for even a moment longer, for fear that the teacher would follow me out the classroom door, I made a beeline for the front of the school. No one tried to stop me. No one said a word as I left the campus and started walking down the street.

It didn't take me long to realize that I had no idea where I was going. I didn't know where my house was. I stopped in my tracks. Spotting the park, I walked over and climbed onto one of the picnic tables, planting my feet on the bench below me. I needed time to think. I needed time to sort out what was going on.

Where did I live? And why didn't I know the answer to that? Had I bumped my head on something and gotten amnesia? Was amnesia even a real thing? I knew that I was in a middle school though. So there was that. At least my mind wasn't completely erased from reality.

It was a warm, sunny day. Yet I was freezing. I wrapped my arms around in front of my chest, once again, in an attempt to get warm. There was no reason for me to be freezing.

That's when the forest jumped into my consciousness. Somehow I knew that I had just left the forest. And someone had been chasing me. But who? I didn't seem to know the answer to that question. My body involuntarily shivered in response to it all. Though I knew somehow that I had just left the forest, I also knew that it couldn't be possible. I remembered being bruised and bloody, and barefoot. I was none of those things at the moment.

A picture flashed in my mind. "Oh god." I was in a hole and being buried alive by rocks and mud. Tears flowed freely down my face. I wiped them away with the back of my hand.

If someone was just chasing me through the forest, and I was trapped in a huge hole somewhere, how did I end up sitting in a middle school classroom? And why didn't the teacher and other students think it was weird that I was there? I mean, I'm four or five years older than they all were. It seemed as if I would stick out like sore thumb in that classroom. Well, maybe I did. They were all staring at me after all.

I had no idea how long I had been sitting there in the park, when I heard a voice calling my name.

"Georgie, are you all right? Where have you been?"

Looking up, a young girl was approaching. She was pretty, with strawberry hair. I guessed she was about ten years old. I didn't know the young girl...yet, she was familiar somehow.

"Georgie, answer me," the young girl demanded. "What is the matter with you? Mom and Dad have been looking everywhere for you."

My head tilted to the side. "Mom and Dad?"

"Yeah, Mom and Dad. You left school early and they called Mom. Everyone is searching for you. Why would you leave early on the last day of school? I mean, that makes no sense. And why are you just sitting there, looking confused at me?"

"Do I know you?" I asked the girl.

"Georgie, did you hit your head or something?" she retorted without any hesitation.

"I don't know. Maybe."

"Really?" her eyes wide. "I was just kidding. We should go home."

The girl reached for me and I jerked my arm away from her. She dropped her hand to her side and scowled at me.

"Home?" My eyes scanned the horizon. "I don't know where that is. And I don't know who you are." I shivered in the warm sunshine.

The girl in front of me stood staring, without speaking, for a good half minute.

"I'm your sister, that's who I am. And I can't tell if you are joking with me or not," she finally replied.

"My sister? I remember an older girl. Sort of. I think she might be my sister. Do we have another sister? How many of us are there?" I knew my questions probably sounded ludicrous to this girl, but they needed to be asked.

"No, there is no older sister, except you. You really don't remember me?" she asked.

I shook my head. "What's your name?"

"Viv." She hesitated. "I mean, it's really Vivian, but I hate that stupid name. No one dares call me that."

I nodded that time. "Okay, Viv it is. So are there any brothers?"

"No. Just us," she answered. "This is really weird. We should go home, so Mom and Dad can take you to the doctor."

"I can take myself to the doctor. I'm an adult, now that I turned 18."

Viv stood staring at me. When her fists landed on her hips, I knew something was up.

"Okay, you definitely hit your head. You are not anywhere near 18. You're only 13. But nice try." Viv didn't smile as she spoke.

"What? Thirteen! There's no way." I did my best not to screech as I spoke. "I just had my birthday, and I turned 18. You don't know what you are talking about." My eyes narrowed. "Are you really my sister?"

Viv walked over to the picnic table I was sitting on and reached for my purse. "Let me show you something." She began digging through the contents. "Good grief, you have a lot of junk in here. Oh, here it is." She smiled as she triumphantly held up a small compact case.

I watched as she opened it and handed it to me. "Take a look."

Almost afraid of what I might find, I hesitated.

"Here. Take it," she ordered. "You need to see what I see."

I reluctantly reached for the compact. Laying it down in my lap, I covered it with my hands. I was terrified at what I might see. Though there was no rational explanation for what Viv had told me, she didn't seem to be lying. In fact, she obviously wanted me to look in the mirror. I could see in her face that she was telling the truth. But how was that even possible?

CHAPTER 3

I drew in a sharp breath at the reflection looking back at me from that tiny compact mirror.

Though there were only five years separating 18 and 13 years old, there was a huge difference in my appearance. I no longer looked like a somewhat mature 18 year old. I looked like a child. No makeup. Long, straight hair. And I was skinnier than I was the day before. The day that all those rocks came tumbling down on me.

My mother, Ivy, once told me that she had a secret. She said that she had relived her life several times, with the ability to remember and change the outcome each time.

I didn't believe her.

I believe her now.

Some of it was coming back to me. The first time I time traveled, as I call it now, I was only seven years old. I didn't understand at all what was happening to me at the time. I am pretty sure that I drowned in Red Lake on the 4th of July, and came back to life as a five year old. It didn't happen again for many years. But I know it happened.

I once told my mother and brother the story of my drowning. They looked at me funny, and of course, they didn't believe me. Over the years, I kind of put it out of my mind and forgot about it. After a while, I just assumed that it was the imagination of a small child and had never actually happened at all.

Now I know better.

"Oh no," I whimpered. "This can't be happening."

"What can't be happening?"

Startled out of the shock of what I was seeing in the mirror, I looked up toward the voice. It was that girl again. The one who told me she was my little sister. That was one that I still couldn't believe. I had an older sister and brother. Not a little sister.

"Um, who are you again?" I asked, knowing how stupid it sounded, even as it was coming out of my mouth.

"Okay, something is definitely wrong with you." She reached for my hand and I let her take it that time. "Come on. I'm taking you home."

I obliged. What else was I going to do? I didn't know where I lived. I didn't even know where I was. It didn't look like Red Lake, the town I had grown up in.

Looking around at the park I was sitting in, it looked like any other park in small town America. The soft grass was manicured at a perfect three inches. The oak trees were trimmed, nice and neat. Even the sidewalks were pristine. Not a crack to be found.

The two of us walked out of the park together and down the sidewalk. Viv chattered on and on the entire way. I said almost nothing. What was I going to say? I already had her worried about me because I didn't remember her, or where I was.

My mind began to wander as we strolled. Most of what Viv was saying was lost somewhere on that warm summer afternoon. Looking around to get my bearings, this town, or at least this section of town, was quite different than what I was used to in Red Lake. It appeared as if the streets and homes were all perfectly planned out. Instead of the stick straight streets that I was used to, these were gently winding. Kind of meandering, if you will. Even the paint colors of each house seemed to perfectly coordinate with every other house on the block. It was all a little bit odd, certainly not what I was used to. There was a strange vibe to the neighborhood. The whole thing gave me the shivers.

When we came upon a huge house, Viv turned up the walkway. I stood in stunned silence at the enormity of the place.

Viv turned back to me. "You coming?"

"Where are we?"

"Home. Don't you know that?" Viv ran her fingers through her short, strawberry colored hair as she spoke.

"I don't live here." My eyes scanned the building from the front steps to the top. It was three stories high. I had never lived in anything like it. That was something I was positive of.

"Yes you do." She motioned for me to follow her. "Come on, Mom and Dad are waiting for us."

I didn't budge. "Wait, what are their names?"

"Whose names?" she asked.

"You said Mom and Dad," I explained. "What are their actual names?"

"You don't know Mom and Dad's names?"

"No." I was getting irritated with the back and forth, but she was ten years old. So I gave her a bit of latitude. "That's why I asked."

"Beverly and Stan," she replied, ignoring my obvious irritation. "I'm going in. You coming or not?"

Viv didn't wait for a response. She turned and walked up the steps. I had no choice but to follow her. I couldn't very well stand there all day outside on the sidewalk.

The outside, grand as it was, didn't do the place justice. From the moment I walked in, it felt like I was in a castle. The place was enormous. Just the entryway itself, was three stories high. It made the house seem so wide and open.

I stood there, looking up at the skylight, so far over my head. My jaw was probably hanging open. I couldn't help it. I had never seen anything like it in my life. The walls were stone from floor to ceiling, completing the castle look.

It was definitely a place I didn't remember having ever been to before. It seemed like if I had been to a place like this, I would remember it. Especially if I lived there. There was no way. Confusion was clouding up my brain.

"What the heck are you doing?"

Startled out of the shock of it all, I slammed my mouth shut and my eyes met Viv's.

"I…just…I…I don't know." Just wow.

"You're weird. Come on. Follow me."

I complied.

Viv led me down a long hallway, with a couple of turns, until it opened up into a large family type room.

"Oh, Georgie, there you are!" A woman of about 40 jumped off the couch and squeezed me tightly. I didn't hug her back.

A man was also in the room, standing his ground. I assumed he was the man who was supposed to be my father. Another person who I didn't remember at all.

When she let go, and backed up a bit, she stared intently into my eyes. This was it. The moment when they would all tell me that there had been some horrible mistake. I wasn't their daughter. They had no idea who I was.

But that didn't happen.

"Georgie, you scared us all to death. Where in the world have you been?" she asked me.

"I…well…I…"

Before I could say anymore, Viv interrupted. "Yeah, she's been stuttering like that for a while now. I think she hit her head."

The woman looked back at me. "Honey, is that true? Did you hit your head?"

Completely at a loss for words, Viv jumped in once again. "Mom, she said she might have. Maybe we need to take her to the doctor."

"No. I'm fine. I'm just not feeling very good." There was no way that I was going to the doctor.

"Do you want to go to your room and lie down?" the woman, who was supposed to be my mother, asked.

"Yes, thank you."

"Ok, I'll come check on you in a little bit," Beverly said.

Beverly, her husband, and Viv all stood watching me waiting for me to leave. The problem was that I had no idea where my room was. The house was so massive, that I couldn't even begin to guess in what direction to head. My eyes widened. No doubt, I looked terrified. All three of them stood staring at me.

I think Viv figured out what was going on, because she spoke up. "Come on, I'll walk with you. I just want to make sure you get there all right."

I let out a sigh of relief.

Up a flight of stairs and down a long hallway, we finally reached my room. Shock is the only thing that can describe what I saw when I walked in. The room was massive. There was a sitting room that we walked through first. It had a couch and a dresser and a vanity area. But the huge closet was what really caught my attention. My last bedroom was not as large as the closet I was staring into. I stood gawking for a minute or so, before Viv brought me back to reality with her laughter.

"Girl, come on," she giggled. "If you think this closet is something special, wait until you see your actual bedroom."

She wasn't kidding. My bedroom was the most beautiful room I had ever seen in my life. It was pink and white, with ruffled bedding. The room was so large that I felt like I could have a tennis match in there, and still have plenty of room for the spectators.

"Do we share this room?" I asked Viv.

Her eyes lit up with amusement. "No, silly. My room is next door. It's about the same size as this one. But it's definitely not pink."

I liked the pink, and for some reason felt a little bit defensive about her remark, which was odd, since I had never even been in the room before.

I peeled my eyes away from the gorgeous room. "What's wrong with pink?"

She shrugged. "Nothing, I guess. If you're three." Her eyes twinkled.

"Whatever." I walked over and sat on my pink, frilly bedspread. "Now what?"

"What do you mean?" Viv asked with a tilt of her head.

"You know what I mean," I responded. "I told you that I don't remember any of you."

I hadn't mentioned that I was pretty sure I died in that hole I had fallen into. Having no idea what was going on, I kind of kept that part to myself. If I had died, then why was I here? And why was I in a strange house, in a strange city, with a strange family?

"So, what city are we in?"

Viv furrowed her brows in my direction. "You don't know what city we are in?"

Trying my best not to sound exasperated, "That's why I asked. Are we in Red Lake?" I already knew the answer to the question.

"Something is seriously wrong with you," Viv responded. "We are not in Red Lake. That's about a half hour from here."

"Oh." It was all I could mutter out. "I'd like to be alone, if you don't mind." It was a sincere request.

"Yeah, okay." Viv walked out without another word.

I plopped down on my back and stared at the ceiling. I smiled when I realized it had sparkly stars on it, which probably glowed in the dark. How different it was to be 13 years old instead of 18.

An image of my mother flashed in my mind. Not the woman whose house I currently inhabited. I saw Ivy. The only mother I remembered ever having. At least, I think that was her name.

Where was she? At home in Red Lake? Probably. I wondered how she would react to me calling her. For some reason I didn't remember her very well. Just a few flashing images, distorted in my mind. I wondered if they were actual memories or just some crazy dreams. The problem was that I couldn't come up with any concrete memories. I wondered what that meant. Did it mean that I was making everything up? Was Beverly, whatever her last name was, my actual mother? Was I hallucinating the whole experience?

I wasn't sure exactly why, but I was pretty sure I wasn't hallucinating. I was pretty sure that Ivy was my actual mother. So why was I here with this family? And why was I only 13 years old. How in the world did this happen?

CHAPTER 4

I must have been absolutely exhausted, because the next thing I knew, I heard someone calling my name.

My eyes opened with a start, then slammed shut at the bright morning light piercing its way into the room.

"Georgie. Georgie!"

Rolling over to my side, "Mmm, what?"

The voice was young, yet it didn't register with me who it was just yet.

"Georgie, get up. Mom made breakfast."

"Who?" I opened my eyes again, more slowly this time. I scanned the room and the eerie feeling of being in the wrong place, and the wrong time, began to creep over me. "Oh." That's when I remembered the events of the previous day. "Go away. I'm not hungry."

"You better get up," Viv ordered. "Mom made pancakes and she'll get mad if you don't show up for them."

I turned over to see her standing at the side of my bed, hands on hips. "Did you sleep in your school clothes?"

Pulling myself to a seated position, I looked down at my rumpled clothes. "Yeah, I guess I was tired." I really needed a shower. I needed to wash all of the previous day's horror off of me. Looking up into Viv's impatient face, "Where's the bathroom?"

Without a word, she pointed to her left. My gaze followed the line of her finger to find a closed door, not ten feet from where I sat.

"Oh, okay. I'm going to take a shower. I'll be down in a bit."

"Okay, fine. Mom's gonna be mad," Viv told me, with a dramatic flare to her voice.

As she turned and headed to my bedroom door, I responded. "I'm sure she'll get over it," I muttered under my breath.

Her feet stopped dead in their tracks and she spun around to face me. "What did you say?" Her eyes wide and questioning.

"Nothing," shaking my head. "I said nothing."

With a roll of her eyes, Viv turned and walked out the door.

I'm probably going to pay for that one, I thought to myself. Viv seems like a squealer to me.

Twenty minutes later, I had showered, dressed in some jeans and a pink top I found in the closet, and found my way to the dining room. I sat next to Viv, having no idea if there was a specific chair assigned to me or not. There were probably ten empty ones at the table. No one seemed to notice, or care, where I sat.

I said very little during breakfast. Truth was that I didn't have much of an appetite. Again, no one seemed to notice. After breakfast, I got up and wandered around the house. It seemed necessary for me to get to know my surroundings a bit.

The family room that I had first walked into the night before with Viv, was where I found myself a few minutes later. It was strewn with family photos, many of which featured myself. I looked at happy, smiling faces at the beach, at a cabin in the mountains, at someone's birthday party.

The problem was that I didn't remember being at any of those places. And I didn't remember any of the faces smiling alongside me either. Not a single one. What I did remember, was being with another family. There was a mother, me, an older brother, and an older sister. Their faces were a bit blurry in my mind, but they were there. I knew they were. I did my best to clear up those faces, but it wasn't happening. Not yet, anyway. But I knew it would happen. Time was all I needed.

"Hey, Georgie, what are you doing?"

I turned toward the unfamiliar voice and found a boy, of about 13, standing at the entrance of the family room. He was wearing yellow and white swim trunks, and had a towel draped around his neck. His feet were bare.

Suddenly, an image flashed in my mind. Before I had a chance to decipher it, a piercing pain slammed into the center of my forehead. If I hadn't known any better, I could have sworn I had been shot between the eyes.

My hand flew to my forehead and I cried out. As my knees began to buckle, I heard running steps and felt strong arms catch me before I hit the ground. He guided me gently into a seated position on the floor.

"Georgie! What happened?" It was the voice of the boy who only moments prior was standing across the room, smiling at me.

"I...I don't know." I rubbed my forehead as the pain began to subside. "I feel like someone just...hit me in the head."

"No. You were just standing there looking at photos one second. Then you turned to look at me and started to fall. I almost didn't make it in time to catch you," the boy responded.

That's when I looked up into his eyes. They were the most beautiful shade of bright green I had ever seen. For a kid, he was quite cute. He would grow to be a heartbreaker one day. He seemed to be about my current age of 13, which, in my 18 year old brain, was a child.

"Do we know each other?" I asked, fearing that I should not have asked the question.

His brows furrowed. "Georgie, you don't know who I am? It's me, Tommy. Now I'm really worried about you."

"Oh, um." I knew that I needed to backtrack a bit. Until I could figure out what was going on, I kind of needed to play along with everything. "Um, sorry. I just have a piercing headache right now. Can you help me to the couch?"

For a young teen, Tommy was quite strong. He lifted me to a standing position with what seemed like no effort whatsoever. Sitting down on the couch, I needed a few minutes to gather my thoughts.

"Would you mind getting me a glass of water from the kitchen?"

"Sure." He disappeared from sight.

My mind recalled the image that flashed in my head when Tommy had first walked into the room. The image was of him. I was sure of it. We were in a swimming pool, and Viv was with us. Turning toward the backyard windows, there it was. The actual pool in my mind. Because of the swim trunks he showed up in, it was pretty obvious that he was here for the pool.

Had we made previous plans? Or did he just show up out of the blue?

"Here you go."

Tommy walked over and handed me a glass of ice cold water. It was soothing and made me feel a lot better almost immediately.

"Do you know who I am now?"

Watch your answer. You don't want to make anyone suspicious. "Uh, yeah, of course. Sorry about before. I was just confused. You know, with the headache and all. I'm fine now though."

I watched his face for a reaction. It turned from concern to uncertainty, and then finally acceptance. I could see that he believed my story. That was good to know. It was important that people just saw me as the teenage Georgie that they have always known.

What happened next landed me on the floor. A huge wave of memories, I suppose, and images just began to flood my head. It was so overwhelming, that for a moment I honestly thought my head was going to explode. I grabbed my head and screamed. Before I knew it, I was sliding off the couch and onto the floor.

The flashes in my head were of Viv and her parents. There were also other people that I knew. I could see memories of us swimming and going to school and eating meals together. All the things that a family would do. All of a sudden I knew every-thing. This was my family. The family that I didn't remember a few minutes prior.

I even saw images of Tommy, the boy sitting next to me. They played out in my mind as if we were watching a video of my life. He and I walked to school together sometimes.

"Georgie, Georgie! Are you all right?"

It was Tommy's voice that I heard. He was trying to drown out everything in my head. It was starting to work. The images and videos that I could see were fading. Not fading from my memory, just from the onslaught I had just experienced.

I flinched when I felt a cool hand on my shoulder. It was Tommy, shaking me and trying to bring me back to reality. Finally it was over and my eyes opened. I don't know why, but I felt no embarrassment. It was as if Tommy was a brother to me. We were best friends and that is something I just knew to be true.

When I tried to pull myself up to a seated position, I felt Tommy's strong hands grasp my arm and pull me up to the couch. He sat next to me.

"Georgie, what happened? Should I get your mom?"

Shaking my head ever so slightly, "No, no, I'm fine. Really. Can I get a drink of..."

I scanned the table in front of me and that's when I realized that I must have dropped the glass of cold water when my attack happened. There was broken glass all over the floor and water everywhere, including on the shorts I was wearing.

Tommy noticed what I was looking at. "Oh, don't worry about that. I'll clean it up in a minute. First, let me go get you some more water."

Before I had a chance to answer him, Tommy jumped up and ran to the kitchen. It gave me a moment to reflect on what had just happened.

It was almost as if I was born only a minute ago. I remembered everything. I remembered my family. I remembered my friends. But...I also remembered another family. I struggled to recall them. It was as if this new family was erasing the old one from my life. I remembered my other mother was named Ivy. But her face was rapidly disappearing.

I saw long, red, curly hair. But couldn't make out her features. "Please, don't go away," I pleaded, desperately holding onto any bit that I could.

"I'm not going anywhere."

Startled, I jumped up out of my seat. It was Tommy returning with my glass of water. I let out a sigh.

"Be careful," he warned. "There's still broken glass at your feet."

Instinctively, I looked down. Somehow, through everything I had just gone through, I still managed to have sandals on my feet. Good thing I did too. If not, my feet would for sure be torn in shreds by all the glass on the floor. I looked back up at Tommy.

"I don't want to lose them." I spoke without thinking.

Tommy tilted his head. "Lose what?"

"Not 'what', but 'who.' I don't want to lose...never mind. You wouldn't understand." I sat back down on the couch and buried my face in my hands.

Tommy set the glass of water on the coffee table in front of us and plopped down on the couch next to me. I flinched in response. I don't really know why I did that, but I did. I remembered Tommy finally. It wasn't as if we were strangers. But just because I remembered him in my mind, doesn't mean that I still didn't feel a bit of unease. I still felt uncomfortable with the entire situation.

"Okay then," he responded. "Who? Who is it that you don't want to lose?"

"My family." My eyes scanned the photographs scattered about. "My other family."

Tommy scooted about a foot away from me. Not to get away, but to get a better look as he turned toward me. He lifted one leg and folded it underneath the other. It seemed like a very familiar thing to me. As if I had seen him do that a hundred times. Since we were friends, I probably had.

"Georgie, what is going on? Your other family?"

I looked down at my feet. "You wouldn't understand. No one would."

Tommy reached over and with just his index finger under my chin, he gently turned my head so that I was facing him. There were those piercing green eyes again. It was such a gentle and loving gesture.

"Hey, Georgie, it's me. You know, your best friend? You can tell me anything. You know that, right?"

Did I know that? Yes, I remembered the two of us being friends. But this was one of those things that I just wasn't sure I could tell him. I mean, this was a life changing secret. How in the world could I explain to him that I just died and came back to life yesterday. He would not understand. No one would.

CHAPTER 5

Taking a hold of his hand, I start heading for the front door. "Come on, let's go for a walk. We can talk then."

I had made the decision to tell Tommy what I knew. Would he believe me? Doubtful. Did it even matter at this point? Yes, I think it did. I needed an ally. I was hoping Tommy could be that person.

Tommy stopped dead in his tracks, releasing my hand from his grip. "Georgie, wait. Do you see what I'm wearing?" He pointed at his yellow swim trunks.

I smiled in response. Yeah, he had on swim trunks. Only swim trunks. No shirt, no shoes. He was not really prepared for going on a walk.

"Yeah, okay," I responded. "How about we go sit by the pool? That's what you came over for anyway, didn't you?"

Nodding, Tommy turned and headed for the back door. I followed. Once we were seated in a couple of beach chairs next to the pool, I hesitated. I hadn't really thought through what I was going to say. I needed to find a way to say it without sounding like a lunatic. Tommy might have been my best friend, but that didn't mean he would believe every crazy thing that came out of my mouth.

Tommy began. "Okay, let's hear it. What's been eating you? I can tell it's big. So, out with it."

I smiled, remembering Tommy's fun personality. He pulled no punches, as they say. He was blunt, but not in a rude way. He was very likable and had many friends. I was the lucky one to say that I was his best friend.

"Well, all right," I began. "This is going to sound completely insane, but please hear me out, okay?"

Tommy nodded. "You know I will." He sounded so much more mature than the 13 year old that he was.

"Okay, here goes."

Before saying anything, I looked at Tommy, deep into his eyes. I could see curiosity, but also understanding. At that moment, I knew that I could trust him. He was probably the only one on the planet that I could actually trust.

"I don't belong here," I began.

"What do you..." I shot my hand up to interrupt him.

"Just let me finish, please," I asked.

Tommy nodded in response.

"Like I said, I don't belong here. Just yesterday, I was in a deep hole, a cavern-like place, with water running through it. I think it may have been the sinkhole in Red Lake. You know the one that people talk about?" I raised my eyebrows questioningly.

"Yeah, I know the place. I've been there with my friends," he responded.

"You have? When? Oh, never mind," I told him. "It doesn't matter. Anyway, I was there and the wall caved in on me and I'm pretty sure I died."

"You what? Are you being serious with me right now?" Tommy was shaking his head in my direction. It was obvious what he was thinking.

"Yes, I am being serious right now. Please just listen?"

"Okay, go ahead." Tommy leaned back in his chair to hear my story.

"The reason why I think I died is because I was 18 years old yesterday, and living with another family. At least I think I was. Living with the family that is. I know I was 18. Then I suddenly found myself sitting in a middle school classroom with everybody staring at me."

I stopped speaking to gauge Tommy's reaction. It was pretty much what I expected. Disbelief. Maybe even some mistrust. He probably thought I was playing a joke on him. I mean, who wouldn't think that?

"Are you still with me?" I asked, fearing the answer.

"Yeah, I guess," he responded with a bit of trepidation in his voice. "What is this all about? What are you trying to pull here?"

Yep, he didn't believe me. Well, I had gone this far and really had no choice but to continue. I needed to figure out how to make him believe me.

"I know how it sounds. Really I do. But please bear with me. Okay?" It almost sounded like I was pleading. In a way, I was.

"Yeah, okay."

"When I found myself in that classroom, I bolted. I went to the park, and just sat there, kind of confused. Viv found me a while later and brought me here. I didn't remember any of this family. None of them," I explained. "Then all of a sudden, after I saw you, memories started flooding back. I remembered everything. This family. You. Everything. But somehow, it still seems like it happened to someone else. It's as if a movie is playing in my head."

"So, if you remember everything and everyone, what's the problem? Obviously, that whole thing didn't happen. You were dreaming, or hallucinating, or something. I don't know."

Tommy was trying his best to tie this whole thing into a neat little bow.

"No, you don't understand," I continued. "It did all happen. All of it. I know it did. I had another family yesterday. My mother's name is Ivy, but that's all I know. I think there was an older brother and sister, but I don't remember their names now. And now, my memories of all of them are beginning to fade." I brushed a tear from my cheek with the back of my hand.

Tommy was beginning to squirm in his seat on the chair next to me. He seemed uncomfortable with the whole situation. What was I to expect from a 13 year old?

I began to plead. I needed an ally more than he would ever know. "Please, Tommy, you have to believe me. I swear on my life that I'm telling the truth. I just don't know how to prove it."

"Let's see if we can find that other family of yours. Then I might believe you. Maybe," he offered.

I thought about that for a moment. "Yeah, but the problem is that I don't know their last name. The only name I have is Ivy. And I'm almost positive that I lived in Red Lake."

"Well Red Lake is not that big," Tommy responded. "There can't be that many Ivy's living there. It's not that common of a name."

"Are you going to take me to the mall or not?"

We both turned toward the hallway to see Viv emerging. She was dressed for a day out. A day at the mall.

"What are you talking about?" I asked her. "Did we have plans?"

"Yes, we had plans. You forgot already?" She set her feet wider apart and propped one hand on her right hip. When she raised her eyebrows, I knew she meant business.

"The mall? Where is the nearest one?" I asked. That was something I didn't remember.

"Over in Red Lake. You know that," Viv spouted.

"Oh." It was all I could say.

"Well?" Viv asked, shifting her hips to the left.

"Well what?" I answered. "You know I can't drive."

"Mom said she would drop us off," Viv told me. "But not by myself. She said you have to go."

I looked over at Tommy, who shrugged my way.

"Okay fine," I told my new little sister. "Let me go get ready."

I stood up. Tommy followed suit.

"Looks like swimming is out today," he added to the conversation, his shoulders slumping just a bit. "I'm going home. Call me when you get back. K?"

I nodded. "Okay." Leaning over to whisper to him, I added, "Please think about what I told you. I swear every word is true."

Tommy nodded on his way out.

About an hour later, our mother dropped us off at the Red Lake Mall, right in front of the huge bookstore near the entrance. Apparently she knew that it was my favorite store in the entire mall. I could spend hours browsing through the place, searching for just the right book. Small town dramas were my favorite.

The moment our mother was out of sight, Viv took off.

"I know you are going to spend the next two hours in the bookstore," she hollered over her shoulder. "I'm going in the mall and will come find you later."

I lost sight of her before I even had a chance to answer. I shrugged. She wasn't wrong. I had no desire to walk through the mall and look at clothes. That just was not my thing. I know I might be unusual for a teenager. Fine with me. I headed inside the bookstore.

I couldn't help but smile the moment I walked in. The place was massive. I couldn't imagine any book that I wanted that wouldn't be there. I immediately headed to the drama section.

As I browsed through the books, I couldn't help but think about my old family. Were they actually real? I could barely picture my mother anymore. I almost began to think that I hallucinated the whole thing. I struggled to keep my memories. At least I hoped that's what they were.

Feeling a chill run up my spine, I had the strangest sensation that someone was watching me. I don't know why that bothered me. It had to be Viv. Who else would it be?

I turned to look down the aisle to see who might be near me. There was no one. I walked to the end and looked down the cross aisle. Still no one. Well, I figured I was just imagining things.

A few minutes later, there was that sensation again. Someone was watching me. I could feel it deep down in my bones. Feeling a tap tap on my right shoulder, I jumped, the books in my arms scattering around my feet.

CHAPTER 6

Barely noticing the books at my feet, I spun around to find a young girl with wide eyes standing before me. She was a pretty brunette, several years older than I currently was. Maybe 19 or 20. I had no idea who she was, yet she was familiar at the same time.

"Hi," the girl said to me, backing up just a bit.

"Hi."

Should I start asking her questions? Like, 'Do I know you?' That might be weird if we were friends in this lifetime. But she was a lot older than I was. I doubted that we were friends. We could know each other some other way though. She could be the sister of a friend of mine. No telling. Everything was just so out of whack for me at the moment.

The girl stood staring at me for what seemed like an eternity. It started making me feel a bit uncomfortable. I shifted from foot to foot.

"You look familiar," she finally spoke.

"I do?" She kind of looked familiar to me too.

"Yeah," the girl responded. "What is your name?"

"Georgie. What's yours?"

She smiled as if she had a secret. "Harper."

Harper? I knew that name. Where did I know it from? Which life did I know it from?

Having no clue what to say next, I kneeled down and began gathering up the books I had dropped a few moments prior. Harper kneeled and picked up two of the books. Standing, she put them on top of the pile in my hands.

Eyeing the load of books I was holding, Harper spoke next. "You must really like to read."

Nodding, "I do."

"What kind of books do you like?" she asked.

Shrugging one shoulder, "Mostly small town dramas. Oh and true crime stories. I can't seem to get enough of them."

"Me too. I love those," she told me with a smile.

She was a pretty girl. I just wished I knew where I knew her from.

"So, how do you think we know each other?" I asked. "I need to set these books down. They're super heavy."

I walked over to a table nearby and set the entire stack down. Harper followed me. Rubbing my arms, to get the circulation going again, or more likely, just because I was a bit nervous, I looked up to the girl for an answer to my question.

"Do you really think we know each other?" I asked again.

She nodded. "Yes. But I'm not sure if I'm right. I don't know if I should tell you."

My face scrunched up. "Why wouldn't you tell me?"

"Are you adopted?" she blurted out.

"What? No." I hesitated for a minute. I didn't actually know the answer. I had just had a gut reaction to the question. It had never occurred to me that I might be adopted. "I don't think so. No, I'm sure I'm not." I wasn't sure at all. "Why would you ask me that?"

My voice was defensive. There was no way around it. Some

stranger comes up to me in a bookstore and starts asking me if I'm adopted. That was weird no matter how you looked at it.

Harper looked down at the table where my books were perched. "Can we sit down? I think you really need to hear what I have to say."

"Um, okay, I guess." What was the harm? Even if this girl was a few rocks short of a quarry, we were in a public place. There was nothing she could do to me in a bookstore.

Once seated, she began. "I think it's possible, maybe, that you are my little sister."

My eyes widened. "What? How is that possible? I only have one sister and she's three years younger than I am."

"Yeah, that's what I figured," Harper responded. "I don't mean the family you are living with. I mean my family. I think you may be my little sister who was kidnapped ten years ago." She leaned back in her chair and bit her lower lip, waiting for my reaction.

Drawing in a quick breath, I needed a moment to respond to that. "Why would you think that? I mean, I would have only been 8..um 3 years old ten years ago." I needed to remember that I was only 13 years old in this lifetime.

"Yeah, I know. The thing is that when I first saw you walk into this store," she scanned the room without moving her head, "I immediately noticed that you look a lot like my missing little sister. Just older. And you look a lot like my mother."

I started to stand. This was ridiculous. Harper's hand shot out and took my hand. I looked down and she pulled her hand away from mine.

"Sorry. Please, just hear me out. There's more, and I think you may start to agree with me once you hear it."

There was a sadness to her eyes that told me she believed everything she was saying. I relented and sat back down.

"Thank you. So, like I said, the first thing I noticed was that you look a lot like I remember my little sister looking. And, of course, we have pictures of her all over the house."

"I'm sure lots of little kids look similar," I told her.

She shrugged. "Maybe. But now that you are older, you look a lot like my mother. You have the same red hair. And those eyes. You are the only one who got those pretty green eyes. Exactly like my mom's."

I looked away. I needed time to think. I still kind of remembered another family. But their faces and names had mostly faded. The name Harper was vaguely familiar. But I couldn't remember for sure from where. This girl was probably just mistaken.

"I don't know. This all sounds like just some sort of coincidence. The chances of…"

She cut me off with a flash of her palm in the air. "Wait, please. I have more to tell you."

I let out an exasperated sigh. It didn't go unnoticed by Harper.

"My little sister's name was Georgie."

I sat straight up in my seat. "What? Is this for real?"

She nodded. "One hundred percent real. This can't be a coincidence. It just can't be."

That's when I dared ask the question. But I needed to know. "What is your mother's name?"

"Ivy Wells."

My head started spinning, and my peripheral vision was fading. When my breathing became labored, I grabbed Harper's arm in a desperate attempt to keep from passing out. She grabbed both of my arms and held me steady.

"Georgie. Georgie! Are you all right? Do you want some water?"

My vision was coming back and I nodded. Water might actually help. She stood up, but hesitated and didn't release me.

I nodded. "It's okay, you can go. I'll be all right."

"Well, if you're sure." She slowly released my arms and waited a minute longer to make sure I really was okay. "I'll be right back. Don't go anywhere." She took off like a shot.

In no more than 30 seconds, Harper returned with two small paper cups spilling over with water. She set them on the table in front of me. I gulped the first one down. The liquid was cool to my throat and I began feeling better right away. I did the same with the second one. By then, my head was clearing and my breathing was back to normal. Placing the second cup inside the first, I swiped the drops of water that had spilled over, with just a brush of my forearm. It left a damp streak across the table. Harper sat back down next to me.

"Are you sure you're okay?" she asked, a pained gaze on her face. "Did I cause this? I'm so sorry."

Looking up into Harper's brown eyes, I saw something familiar, and I somehow knew that what she was telling me was the truth. There was an older sister somewhere in the back of my mind, and I think we just found each other.

"No, it's okay." I patted the back of her hand, which was lying on the table between us. "I'm starting to believe you. I don't remember you all very much, but I know the name Ivy."

"I'm glad you're feeling better. The color is starting to come back into your face. Your face blanched when I told you my mother's name."

"Yeah, I'm sure it did. Here's the thing. I remember a woman named Ivy, with red hair. I thought she might be my mother," I told her. "But I wasn't positive. I was so young."

"You were only three when you were taken," Harper explained.

"Do you know who took me?"

She shook her head slightly. "No clue. But now I'm guessing it was the people who you now live with, who you think are your family."

I thought about those people. I couldn't imagine them doing

something like that. Could they? My memories of them had come back, but still, I didn't feel as if I knew them. Were they that type of people? I really didn't know. But it was something that I needed to find out.

"How was I kidnapped? I mean, what happened?" I asked, genuinely curious.

Harper took a deep breath and let it out slowly, before she began speaking. "You know, I was only ten years old at the time, but I remember it like it just happened. We were having a picnic..."

An image, a memory actually, swept through my mind and I stopped Harper from speaking. "Wait. Were we at a lake?"

"Yes, we were at Red Lake, right on the shore," she told me. "Do you remember that?"

"Yeah, I think so. I remember running and laughing and eating chicken wings."

"Oh wow. I can't believe you remember that. We were having chicken wings. And potato salad. This is just crazy," Harper smiled.

"And I remember a man. He was really tall, with dark hair. I climbed into his car to go get something he said we forgot. I knew him, I think. At least I don't remember being afraid of him. I'm not even positive if he was the kidnapper. I just remember getting into his car. I can't even be sure it was the same day. But I had on the same pink dress I was wearing at the picnic. I'm pretty sure of that." It all came out without me thinking about what I was saying. Until that moment, I had no idea that I knew or remembered any of that.

"Yes! You did have on a pink dress. Mom bought it for you the day before. I'm not sure who that man was. I know lots of people with dark hair. We'll have to work on figuring that out. He isn't someone you know now?" she asked.

"I just don't know. I might know him. His face is blurry in my memory. I was so little. Maybe it will come back to me later." I searched my memory, but could not bring him up again. He had only been there for a moment in my head.

"Oh my god, this is insane. Mom is going to freak out!" Harper exclaimed. "We need to go see her." Harper stood. She looked at me expectantly.

I stayed seated. "Whoa, wait a minute." I held up my palm toward her. "I can't go see her. Not right now anyway. No. Sorry."

"What? Why not? Don't you want to see your mother?" Harper gave me a slow, disbelieving head shake. I could see the pain in her face.

"The thing is, that I have a family now. A family that raised me and loved me. I'm not sure what to do about that." I knew how insane that sounded. Like I wanted to stay with my kidnappers. But that wasn't it at all. I was terrified of seeing Ivy. She was my real mother. She was the one who probably cried herself to sleep for a very long time after I disappeared. How was I going to handle seeing her again? And perhaps more importantly, how was she going to handle seeing me again?

CHAPTER 7

"Are you going to answer me? Georgie! Are you listening to me?"

Harper's raised voice jolted me out of my daydream.

"Oh, sorry. Um, you know, I can't go right now. They are expecting me back home." The hitch in my voice had to have given away the little white lie I just told to my newfound sister.

Harper sat back down beside me. "Are you kidding me? You don't actually expect to go back to those kidnappers, do you?"

I could see where she was coming from. It did sound ludicrous that I wanted to go back to them. But it was the only thing I could do at the moment. I didn't have the nerve to face Ivy. My only response was a weak, one shouldered shrug. At least I was acting like a 13 year old.

In a much softer voice this time, Harper continued speaking. "We live over on Centre Ct, here in Red Lake. So where do you live? You never said."

Though I could tell she was trying her best to sound nonchalant about the whole thing, it was painfully obvious that she was prying me for information. There was no way in hell I was going to tell her where I lived. The police would probably be at the house before I even arrived home.

I looked up at the bookstore ceiling, so far above our heads, just as the air conditioning kicked in. Rubbing my left arm, I could feel goosebumps rising.

"It's kind of chilly in here. I'm going to go get my sweater. My little sister has it." I jumped up out of my chair. "Wait here. I'll be right back."

"Okay, hurry up," she called after me.

I had no intention of returning. Harper seemed like a nice enough person, but I was absolutely terrified of meeting her entire family. My entire family.

I bolted out of the bookstore and straight into the mall. It took me about a half hour, but I finally found Viv. She was in a tween clothing store, right outside the dressing rooms, in front of a mirror, trying on a cute blue and white pinstriped blouse. It looked adorable on her.

Grabbing her by the arm, "Viv, go change out of that, we have to go."

She jerked her arm away from me. "Go where? No we don't. I'm shopping." The scowl on her face told me that she wasn't going to be easy to convince.

I leaned down to her left ear and whispered. "My other sister is here."

Viv pulled away and looked me in the eyes. "Your what? I'm your only sister. Did you hit your head again?" Viv continued checking herself out in the mirror. In essence, dismissing me.

"You know what I mean. The one from my other family that I told you about. And stop asking me if I hit my head."

"I thought you were just kidding about that. Or you were just confused when I found you in the park."

"No, I wasn't...well, yeah, I was a bit confused in the park. But I'm not now. Come on, we have to go," I urged.

With an exasperated 'ugh,' Viv started toward the dressing

room she was standing outside of. "Fine. Give me a minute to change. Then you better tell me everything. And I mean everything." Her wide eyes told me that she meant business.

I kept my eyes pinned on the front entrance of the store, while Viv was changing. Hiding behind a clothes rack was not my finest moment, but there was no way that I wanted to be spotted by Harper. By then, she must be wandering the mall, wondering what had happened to me.

No sign of Harper. But it was a big mall, and she could be anywhere.

"Hurry up!" I whispered as loudly as possible through the dressing room door.

"Okay, okay, I'm coming. Is it all right with you if I tie my shoes first?"

"Yes, just be quick about it," I rushed.

The door opened just a bit. I yanked it open and grabbed Viv by her t-shirt sleeve. "Come on."

Swiping her hand up between mine and the sleeve, she managed to break free of my grip. "Would you just calm down? I'm coming. And this better be good."

Stopping abruptly at the shop exit into the mall, Viv ran smack into my back.

"What are you doing?" The sharp tone that came from her told me that I was on a short leash.

"Sorry. I just wanted to make sure she wasn't right outside."

"Who?" Viv asked.

"My sister. I told you that." I was the one starting to get annoyed.

"You don't have any sister, but me," Viv said, once again.

"Yes, I do…oh shoot, there she is."

I pushed Viv back into the store and behind a rack of bikinis. It wasn't the best hiding place, but it was the closest. I watched Harper scanning the stores as she walked by. Once she passed our store, I crept out from behind the rack and peeked around the corner to where she had headed. She never turned around.

For the next several minutes, Viv and I followed Harper at a safe distance. We managed to stay behind herds of people wandering through the main aisle of the mall. Eventually, Harper headed for the exit. Clearly, she had given up.

"Call Mom. We need to get out of here," I ordered Viv.

While we waited for our mother to drive over to Red Lake, the two of us sat down at the food court and I recounted my version of what had happened to me. From the moment that I found myself alone and afraid, running through the woods, to the predicament I had found myself in at the Red Lake mall.

Viv sat quietly during my entire story, which is something I have come to know about her as completely uncharacteristic. The girl is a talker. If I have to be in a strange place, with a strange family, I'm glad Viv was with me.

"Well, what do you think?" I asked, fearing her answer.

"I believe you."

"You what?" There was no way she could believe such an insane story.

"Georgie, we have been sisters for a long time. I know you well enough to know that you don't lie to me. I also know that you have been acting weird. Something is definitely going on with you. So, I guess I believe you."

I reached over and hugged her. I couldn't help it. There was finally someone who believed me.

"You can't tell anyone about this, okay?" It was more of an order, than a question. "No one will believe you anyway."

"Okay, I won't," Viv replied.

"Oh, except Tommy. I told him already," I added.

Even after I recounted my story, I barely looked at Viv. I kept my eyes on the people around us. I wanted to make sure Harper did not return to look for me. Even worse, what if she showed up with Ivy. I was not prepared for that.

"What are you looking at?" When I lowered my eyes and looked at Viv, she was giving me a glare.

"Sorry. I just wanted to make sure that Harper didn't come back." After that, I did my best to look at Viv and not around me. I wanted to make sure she knew that she was important to me.

"Why did you tell Tommy?" Viv asked me. "I was the one you should have told first." The look on her face was hurt. Maybe even betrayal. I was her big sister and she counted on me to always tell her everything.

"Because he's my best friend," I responded. After moment's hesitation, "at least I think he is. I'm sorry, I just don't know for sure what is going on. I remember us being friends." Viv's face had not changed. She didn't like any of it.

"But I'm your sister. Shouldn't I be the first person you tell about everything? I always was before." At ten years old, her words came out a bit whiney.

I nodded. She was right. She was my sister and should always be the first person I confide in. "Yes, I promise that you will be the one I tell everything to. OK with you?"

"Yeah."

She did not look convinced.

"Oh, there's Mom," Viv told me, jumping up and heading for the exit. I gave chase.

Once home, I needed to figure out what I was going to do next. There were a few options that I could think of. Stay where I was, and go on with my life, was one option. This was unlikely. Besides, Harper was bound to tell Ivy that she talked to me. They would come looking for me. That was something I was sure of.

Option two. Go see Ivy and Harper. She already told me the street they live on. Red Lake was not that big of a town. Finding them would not be difficult. The only problem with this option was that I was terrified of facing them. What would I say?

Would they want me? Yes, I'm sure they would. Would they blubber all over me? Yes, they would probably do that too.

But, how in the world would I explain where I've been all this time? I don't even know myself. Yes, like I said before, I remember everybody, but none of it seems real. The only thing that seems real, is my memory from a few days ago when I was being buried alive in the sinkhole. That's the only thing I'm pretty sure actually happened. The rest of it just seems like distant memories that I cannot confirm in any positive way.

I decided where I needed to begin.

CHAPTER 8

Walking into the kitchen, I found my fake parents, Beverly and Stan, making dinner together. Now that I think about it, that's not a very nice name for them. But, for the time being I didn't know if they were kidnappers or not.

"Oh hi, honey," Stan said, when he noticed I was standing on the other side of the bar, watching them.

"I know you aren't my real parents," I blurted out, immediately regretting it. Some finesse probably would have been the better way to approach the subject.

Beverly gasped. An overreaction, as far as I was concerned. They both turned to look at me. Stan appeared calm, as if I had just ask him to add eggs to the grocery list. Though I had only been in this house for a couple of days, I had come to know Stan as the calm one. Not easily rattled.

Beverly, on the other hand, was easily surprised. She was jumpy, and would practically hit the ceiling if someone walked into the room when she wasn't expecting them. Even in the short few days I had been in this lifetime, it was an obvious personality trait about her.

"Where on earth did you get that idea?" Beverly asked, once

she caught her breath. But it was too late to pretend. Her initial reaction said it all.

Stan looked over at her. In only a few short seconds, he conveyed to her what looked to me like 'Beverly, the jig is up. No need to pretend anymore.' And he did it all without saying a single word.

Her shoulders slumped and she looked down at the floor. There was no doubt in my mind at that moment that I was about to hear a story from them. The pace of my heart quickened in anticipation.

Stan walked over and put his arm around my shoulders. "Honey, where did you hear that?"

"Are you saying it's not true?" I asked.

"No, not at all. We are your adoptive parents. That is true," he replied with a bit of a hitch to his voice. "I just want to know how you found out."

"Um..." How was I going to answer that question? "A friend told me." Lame.

Beverly chimed in. "What friend? No one knows, but us."

"I would...rather not say," I told her. "It was told to me in confidence."

Stan removed his arm from my shoulders and walked over to stand next to his wife. It became a gesture of solidarity.

"Young lady," Beverly's voice became high pitched and agitated, "tell us how you found out."

"No." I crossed my arms, like a 13 year old having a fight with her parents would do.

"Georgie!" Beverly yelled. "Tell us..."

Stan cut her off. "Bev, leave her alone. It doesn't matter anymore. She knows the truth." He was the voice of reason.

"Was I kidnapped?" I was still blurting things out. It's what girls my age did.

Both gave me wide eyes. "What? No!" Beverly responded first. "Why in the world would you think that?"

"Because that's what I was told. I was told that when I was three years old, you grabbed me from a picnic in Red Lake."

"We did no such thing!" Beverly wheezed. I thought she was going to have a panic attack.

"She's right, honey," Stan added. "We would never do something like that."

"Then where did I come from?"

"An adoption agency," Stan answered. "Your biological mother was a drug addict and couldn't take care of you."

"That's not true! Why would you say that!" I screamed. I couldn't help myself. There was no way that I could let them talk about my mother like that. Ivy was a good mother. Not that I really remembered. But I met Harper, and she seemed perfectly fine.

"Okay, okay, calm down now." Stan lowered his voice to barely more than a whisper. It did have a calming effect on me. "Georgie, it is true. We did adopt you through an agency. I swear it's true."

"Then how come my sister, Harper, told me that she remembered the day that I was stolen from the picnic?" Narrowing my eyes, I glared at the two of them while they stood processing what I had just said.

"Your sister?" Beverly asked. "Georgie, what are you talking about? I don't understand."

"Yes you do. I just told you. I have an older sister, she's 20, and I met with her. She told me all about the kidnapping. So, why are you lying to me?" My words were harsh. It wasn't my intention, but it still came out that way. I really didn't know how else to have this conversation.

"When did you meet with her?" Beverly asked me.

"Today at the mall."

"Did Viv meet her too?" Beverly questioned. Her face was ashen.

"No. Just me. Viv was shopping on her own when I met with Harper." I hoped I didn't just get Viv into trouble.

In a deadpan voice, Beverly responded. "I see."

"Uh, Georgie," Stan cut in. "How did you find this Harper person?"

"I didn't. She found me. I was in the bookstore and she recognized me, I guess. She walked up and started talking to me. After comparing notes, it was obvious to the two of us that we were sisters."

Stan tilted his head as he looked at me. "I don't know, Georgie. This could be some sort of scam. Did she ask you where we lived? Or if you have any money? We are pretty well off, you know."

"No! She didn't ask for money! Are you being serious with me right now?" I couldn't believe that he accused my sister of wanting to scam us for money.

"Sounds like your father hit a nerve," Beverly interjected, much calmer by this point. "She did ask you for money, didn't she?"

"No, she did not." My voice was steady, but angry.

"Then what did she say to you, Georgie?" Beverly wanted to know. "She asked where we live, didn't she? Did you tell her?"

"Um, no. I didn't tell her where we live."

The thing is, she did ask where we lived. But I thought it was just curiosity. There was no way she wanted to get money out of me. Was there? I thought for a moment. No, I was pretty convinced that she was just my older sister and wanted to know where I lived. She loved me, and wanted to keep track of me. There was nothing wrong with that.

"Why did you lie to me?" I asked. "You made me think that I was yours."

"You are ours, honey," Stan replied, his voice sincere. "It doesn't matter to us that you are not our biological child. You are our daughter. That's all that matters."

His words had little effect on me. "You didn't answer my question. And that isn't all that matters. I was kidnapped, and I need to know how that happened."

"Georgie," Beverly chimed in, "you are still very young. We had every intention of telling you when you are older. And honey, you weren't kidnapped."

"Mmm, hmm." What they didn't know, was that I was actually 18 in my previous life. So I felt 18, not like the 13 year old child that they were looking at. "I want to see them."

"Look, sweetie," Beverly walked over and pulled me into a hug. "We love you. And when you are 18, we can help you find your biological family. Okay?"

I pulled out of her embrace. "That's five years from now. There's no way I'm waiting that long. Besides, I know where they live. I can go there right now, if I want to."

Beverly shook her head. "No you can't, young lady."

"Wanna bet?" I might have gone too far that time.

"Georgie!" Stan shouted. It made me jump.

"Why are you all screaming?"

The three of us turned to see Viv standing in the doorway with tears spilling down her face.

"Oh honey, I'm sorry." I ran over and wrapped my arms around her. "You okay?"

"No, I'm not okay." Viv squirmed out of my embrace. "I don't know why you hate us so much and want to leave."

"I don't hate you." I looked at my parents. "I don't hate any of you. I just want to know my real...my biological family," I corrected.

"I don't feel comfortable letting you meet your bio family right now," Stan told me. "You are too young."

"I'm not too young," I whined. "Besides, I've already met my sister, and I didn't disintegrate over it."

"Honey, don't be so dramatic," Beverly chimed in. "And I agree with your father. You are much too young."

"I don't care what you two think. I'm going to find them and talk to them. You can either be on board with that, or not. It's up to you. But you can't stop me."

At that point, I stomped out of the room and headed for my bedroom. I was fully aware that I was acting like a four-year-old spoiled brat, but it didn't matter. This was not my family.

In an office across town, two men sat. One in his plush chair behind his enormous solid oak desk, strewn with work documents. He had never been a neat and tidy person. His secretary often questioned him on how he could ever get any work done. He was an average man, in the looks department anyway. Forty something and beginning to bald. He wore a tailored suit, like he did every day for work. At five foot, ten inches tall, and a good 50 pounds overweight, a few of his suit buttons strained at the stress of keeping his girth contained. He didn't seem to notice.

Though average looking, his intelligence meter was through the roof. He had been a gifted child and that carried over into adulthood. He owned his own business and it did exceptionally well.

The other man sat in the customer chair provided on the other side of the large desk. At six feet and four inches, he was considerably taller than the man he was there to see. He wore blue jeans with a rip in one knee, and a faded t-shirt that had seen better days. He was also in his forties and didn't care what anyone thought of him, or his style of dress. He appeared as if he hadn't shaved in at least four days, or had a haircut in a couple of months. His overall appearance was shaggy.

The tall man's intelligence wasn't much better than his overall look. Not quite average, he got through life on luck and not much else.

The men had known each other for over a decade, yet knew so little about the other. They didn't spend much time in conversation. The tall man was there to do a job. The shorter man was there to provide work for him. The combination worked perfectly for them.

"When you come to my place of business, I would appreciate it if you made a bit more of an effort to dress up, Clyde," the shorter man said. "This is a respectable establishment."

The tall man scanned the room slowly, his gaze focusing on vases and fancy artwork on the walls. He smiled at the thought of sneaking into the place after hours and helping himself to whatever he wanted. Though it had crossed his mind, he hadn't dared actually try it. His employer was a dangerous man.

Clyde shrugged at the remark about his clothing. It wasn't going to change anything. He had no intention of wearing anything he didn't want to wear.

"Why did you summon me here?" Clyde asked.

"We need to talk about something," the businessman announced.

"Yeah, what's that." He scratched his itchy beard.

It wasn't often that he was called into the boss's office. Most of his assignments were done over the phone. He kept a special phone that he had bought at the local liquor store, just for the purpose of talking about jobs that were needed to be done. When he was called into the office, it made him antsy. Nothing good could come from having to show up in person.

He stood and began pacing the room.

"Clyde, what has gotten you so amped up?" the businessman asked of the tall man wandering his office aimlessly.

He stopped and turned toward his boss. "Just wonderin' why you needed me to come down here, that's all."

"What we need to talk about is a sensitive subject. I didn't want to take any chances that someone might be listening over the phone." The businessman unbuttoned his suit jacket, to relieve some of the pressure on his stomach from the snug fitting clothes.

"Who would be listening on my phone?" Clyde asked, as the pacing continued.

Without answering the question, the shorter man continued. "Like I said, it's a sensitive subject. Now let's get to it. Okay with you?"

"Yeah, whatever," Clyde answered.

"Can you please sit down? You're making my neck ache just watching you walk back and forth."

With a slight roll of the eyes, Clyde complied.

"We need to do something about the girl."

CHAPTER 9

"Wanna give me a clue as to what girl we are talking about? There are lots of girls out there," Clyde responded.

"Georgie Taylor."

Clyde knew her well. "Oh, that girl. What about her?"

"She's stirring up trouble. She found out that she is adopted. She's causing a lot of problems at home about it."

"Isn't that typical teenage stuff?" Clyde asked. "She doesn't actually know anything, does she?" Shifting in the sticky leather chair made it squeak. He hated that leather chair. "Can't you buy regular chairs like normal people?" He squirmed again.

The boss looked down at the chair briefly, and back up at Clyde. "Forget the chair, will you? We have more pressing things to deal with."

"Yeah, okay. So how did she find out she was adopted?" Clyde asked.

"Apparently her sister, the one from her original family, recognized her at the mall. They struck up a conversation. It all spiraled downhill from there."

"The sister recognized her, even though she hasn't seen her

since the girl was three?" Clyde was dumbfounded. "They don't even live in the same town."

"Maybe not, but it's close enough to Red Lake to be a problem. I just knew I should have placed her further away," the businessman told Clyde.

"Then why didn't you?" Clyde asked.

The other man narrowed his eyes toward Clyde. "You know why."

Clyde nodded his head ever so slightly. Yeah, he knew why. "How do you know that the girl is causing trouble?" Clyde asked.

"I have eyes out there," the boss explained.

Clyde nodded. He knew his boss all too well, and this did not surprise him in the slightest. "Well, she is where she is. What are we going to do about it now?"

"I think you know what to do," the pudgy man said to Clyde.

"Yeah, okay." Clyde stood to leave, turning back just as he reached the office door. "You absolutely sure about this? I mean, she is…"

The boss raised his thick hand to stop Clyde from what he was about to say. "Yeah, I know who she is. And, yes, I'm absolutely sure."

Without another word, Clyde opened the door and exited the office.

Viv and I decided to walk down to the park the next day. I just needed to get out of the house and have someone to talk to.

"How come you don't want to stay with me?" Viv asked. I could see the sorrow written all over her face.

"Oh sweetie, it's not that. I just want to know my biological family. You wouldn't understand," I tried to explain.

"So, you aren't my real sister." It wasn't a question. It was more of a statement that Viv was trying to work through in her head.

"I am your sister. No, we aren't related by blood, but so what? I love you and you will always be my sister. No matter what," I told her. I meant every word of it too.

"Those people didn't want you," Viv replied. "So Mom and Dad adopted you."

"No, that's not what happened. I was kidnapped from my family when I was three."

Viv stopped in the middle of the sidewalk, and faced me. "Mom and Dad didn't kidnap you!"

I patted her left shoulder. "We don't know that. That's what I'm trying to figure out."

The reason I had not gone to talk to Ivy yet, or get the police involved, was that I was terrified I would end up in foster care. That could take years to sort through. The family I was currently with, seemed like nice enough people. I had lived with them for ten years, and seemed okay, so I figured there was very little chance I was in any imminent danger.

Before I had a chance to say anything further, a sudden chill ran up my spine and it stopped me from responding. I turned and looked around us. That's when I saw two men 40 or 50 feet behind us on the sidewalk. They were just standing there talking to each other. I watched them. While doing so, one of them looked up at me and quickly averted his eyes when he noticed me watching him.

Viv turned to look in the direction my eyes were pointing. "What are you looking at?"

I grabbed her shoulder and spun her back toward me. "Don't look over there. Something's wrong." I took her hand. "Come on, we need to go."

I took her hand and dragged her down the sidewalk, away from the men. I was terrified to look behind me, but I felt it was necessary to know if my perceived threat was actually there.

"Wait, stop!" Viv hollered. "I don't want to run." It came out as a kind of yell and whine at the same time.

She tried to pull her hand out of mine, but I was holding tight.

"Let go!"

I turned to look at my little sister, who was struggling against me while pulling her down the sidewalk. As I did so, I glanced up and saw the two men following us. I could see that they were trying to be inconspicuous about it, but it wasn't working. Even at a distance, I could see that one of them was tall and thin, with scruffy hair and unshaven. The other man was following behind him just a bit and I couldn't really see him.

"Georgie, you're hurting me!" Viv cried.

I slowed down a bit, but refused to stop. "I'm really sorry. But, come on, we have to go."

CHAPTER 10

Suddenly, I made a sharp turn into the park. The grass was much softer and spongier than the sidewalk we had been running on, and slowed us down. Viv was startled at my sudden departure from the sidewalk, and she stumbled as we entered the grassy area.

"Georgie, what is going on!" she managed to yell between crying and gasping for breath at the same time.

I knew I was scaring the poor girl, but I couldn't help it. We could deal with all of that later. I was so engaged in trying to keep Viv from collapsing, and at the same time keeping a safe distance from our pursuers, that I hadn't even noticed we were coming up to the forest. The moment we ran into the thick blanket of trees, I regretted it.

I stopped, dead in my tracks. "Oh crap! Now what?" I looked left and then right, then straight ahead of me. Without turning around, I could hear the thundering footsteps of our pursuers. Yes, even on grass, that's what they sounded like.

Besides the footsteps that were going to overtake us at any moment, the scent of pine trees accosted my senses. It was overwhelming, though a pleasant smell. I hadn't noticed it in town. But the moment I hit the forest, it was there. However, there was no time for taking all of that in. We needed to get to safety.

The footsteps were getting louder. We needed to get moving. Having absolutely no idea which direction to go in, I headed straight into the forest, with a determination unlike anything I had ever experienced before.

Viv was blubbering behind me. She was also starting to lag.

"Viv, please. I will explain all of this soon. Someone is chasing us and we need to get away. Please do your best to keep up with me!"

Out of the corner of my eye I saw her glance over her shoulder. Her eyes widened and her pace quickened. I didn't want to scare the poor girl, but it seemed to be working. She was keeping up with me.

Ten minutes later, we were deep in the forest. And completely lost. When we came across a small cave, a very small cave, we climbed inside. I grabbed some branches and other things I could find quickly and put them in front of the cave entrance. It didn't come anywhere close to hiding the front completely, but it did help. Someone would have to be specifically looking right at it to see the entrance. I felt somewhat confident that we would not be discovered.

We pushed our backs up against the far wall, which was only about eight feet in, and prayed that we would not be seen. Or heard.

Wrapping my arms around my little sister, I did my best to calm her down. She was still sobbing and making way more noise than I was comfortable with. Her sobs echoed off the walls, and I feared anyone within a quarter-mile of the place would be able to hear her.

"Shhh," I whispered gently, putting my index finger up to my lips. "We really need to be quiet."

Viv nodded. She knew I was right.

"Take deep breaths. It'll help calm you." My voice was barely audible, even from a few inches away.

Viv did as I told her, and her sobs reduced to not more than a little whimper.

The small cave made the hair on my arms stand on end. For the first time that day, I felt a chill. Though it was summer time, the cave was cold and had a distinctive smell of dampness. I could even hear water running somewhere. But the cave seemed so small, there really was no where to go exploring. Perhaps that running water was coming from somewhere else that we could not get to. Somewhere behind the thick layers of rock we were leaning on.

Viv snuggled up into my arms, so that she was practically sitting on my lap. "I'm scared, Georgie."

That ten year old sassiness that I had to come to admire about my new sister was gone. At least temporarily it was. It was replaced with a frightened little girl, who just wanted to be home with her mother.

It wasn't long before we heard crunching footsteps getting increasingly louder as our pursuers began closing in on our location. Viv let out a low yelp when something, such as a twig, was stepped on not far from the entrance to our cave. I quickly covered her mouth with my hand. But the deed had already been done. Too late to take it back.

My body tensed in apprehension of our hideout being discovered.

I let out a breath of relief when we heard them continue walking on past the cave. We didn't dare move though. We needed to wait for them to get quite a bit away before we ventured out to try to find our way back home.

About one minute later, the footsteps returned. We heard muffled talking just outside. They seemed to be whispering, which is why we couldn't tell what they were saying. Viv let out a startled cry when the branches I had so carefully placed in front of the entrance were yanked away. Our eyes grew wide as saucers when a tall man knelt down and met our eyes with his.

"Georgie!" Viv grabbed onto me for dear life. I couldn't move.

"Viv, let me go."

I needed to get up. I couldn't possibly defend myself in a sitting position, up against the wall, with Viv squeezing me so tightly. I struggled to get out of her grip.

"Viv, I said let go. I need to get up!" The words came out harsher than I meant them to. But this was life or death. I needed her off of me.

"Hey, I got 'em!" the tall man in front of us yelled out into the forest. Running footsteps echoed off of the trees. In under a minute, there were two sets of eyes staring at us.

"Hello girls," the tall man sneered.

"What do you..wa want?" My voice was shaky.

"You get the little one, and I'll get Georgie," the tall man said to the other one, who didn't look much older than a teenager himself.

The whole escapade that was happening to us was shocking, no doubt. But the thing that surprised me the most was that he knew my name. I'm sure my mouth hung open when that happened.

"Who are you?" My voice still shaky. I felt no confidence in my question and I'm sure that showed through.

"Your worst nightmare, that's who."

We both screamed as they clumsily climbed into the cave after us.

CHAPTER 11

The younger man grabbed Viv first. She kicked and clawed at him like her life depended on it. And it probably did.

I wanted nothing more than to come to her rescue, but I had someone to fight off myself. Just as he reached for me, I doubled up my fist and slammed it into his nose as hard as I could, my eyes closed the entire time.

The tall man stumbled backwards grabbing his nose, letting out a string of curses. "Dammit! You bitch!"

Even in the dim cave, I could see blood pouring from his nose. He backed all the way out and disappeared around the corner. I couldn't worry about him anymore. I turned my attention toward Viv and her attacker.

I jumped on the back of the teenage boy. It didn't take long for him to realize that he had a big problem on his hands. He could barely keep hold of Viv while trying to throw me off of his back at the same time.

"Clyde! Where the hell are you! Get these bitches off of me!" he screamed.

No one answered.

"Clyde!"

"Okay, okay, I'm coming."

Strong arms grabbed me from behind, wrapping around my waist and yanking me off of the teenage boy. My arms and legs flailed in the air in an attempt to shake myself loose of him.

"Let me go!" I screamed. My words reverberated off the cave walls. The entire place seemed to shudder. A fleeting thought crossed my mind. It was of rocks falling and crushing us, burying all of us alive.

The moment the man finally set me down on my feet, releasing me as he did so, those thoughts were replaced with anger. I was enraged that he and his friend had the audacity to come after us. Having no actual clue as to what they were planning to do, I knew that it was up to me to defend myself. And my little sister, who I could see still struggling with her captor.

I immediately spun around to face Clyde. That's the name I had heard the younger man call him. Instinctively, he backed up two paces, probably to keep me from slugging him in the face again. A second blow to his nose would probably be his undoing.

Wanting nothing more than to bloody his nose all over again, all I could think of was Viv. I could hear her screaming and fighting the boy with all the might she had. The girl was a scrapper, but she was no match for a boy several years older than she was. He looked young, but he could easily have been in his twenties.

I turned toward their fight. I grabbed a handful of his hair and held on tight, twisting his head around at an impossible angle. He had no choice but to let Viv go and concentrate on me. I heard her land with a thump on the cave floor. The boy reached up and tried to get my hands out of his hair, screaming the entire time.

"Son of a bitch! Let me go! That fucking hurts!"

He tried reaching for my hair, but couldn't get a grip on it. I kept moving around out of his reach. He was bent over with his head twisted and he just had no way of getting a good handful of my hair. No doubt we looked like a couple of 12-year-old girls having a hair pulling fight.

Even in the middle of a fight for my life, I could hear Viv sobbing my name. "Georgie!"

With no chance of getting us away from the two men, I had to ignore Viv and concentrate on my own struggle.

After what seemed like an eternity of the two of us fighting, once again, Clyde grabbed me around the waist and pulled me into the air. The problem with this scenario was that my fingers were still deeply entwined with the teen's hair. He began shouting as chunks of his hair began coming out. He somehow managed to twist around and kick me in the stomach. It knocked the wind out of me and I lost my grip on him.

He stood, rubbing his head. "Bitch, I'm going to kill you." It was said in such a calm manner, that it was more eerie than if he had screamed it at me.

Clyde threw me to the ground, face and arms scraping the rough rock and dirt floor. A moment later, I could feel the blood dripping down my face and arms.

"Georgie!" Viv continued wailing.

Turning to face her once again, I found her huddled in the corner, with tears and snot running down her face. The poor girl was hysterical. I started to crawl toward her. She needed comforting. At the moment, the two men behind me were speaking amongst themselves, leaving me alone.

I saw some movement out of the corner of my eye and watched as Viv's eyes also followed that movement. I continued inching closer and closer to my little sister.

Suddenly, Viv let out an ear piercing scream. "Nooooo!"

That was the last thing I heard. I felt something crush my skull, just as everything went black.

PART 2

CHAPTER 1

"Noooo!" I screamed, opening my eyes simultaneously.

I found myself sitting at the dining room table with several other people, and every pair of eyes was on me. A couple of them snickered under their breaths, but most people had concern in their eyes.

I was having a hard time breathing and became lightheaded. I grabbed onto the arms of the chair I was sitting on and hung on for dear life. My skin felt cold and clammy.

"Georgie, are you all right?" It was Beverly, my adoptive mother.

I leapt out of my chair. "How did I get here?" I put my right hand over my heart and felt it racing. Stars begin dancing around my eyes and I grabbed onto the table to keep from passing out.

"Georgie, what are you doing?" Stan asked.

I took a deep breath. "Where is he?" My voice was frantic sounding, as I jerked my head around, looking at the faces around me. I wasn't even positive who it was I was looking for.

"Who, Georgie?" Viv got up from her chair next to mine and patted me on the back.

She was taller. What? No, it must be my imagination. She couldn't have possibly grown a few inches over the last couple of hours. Or however long it had been since we...oh god, the cave. It all came flooding back to me. I spun around, half expecting to see our two attackers standing behind me. In my rational mind, I knew that was ridiculous. We were sitting down having dinner. What the hell was going on?

I turned back toward all the questioning eyes. I scanned everyone sitting at the table. There were my parents and Viv, of course. Tommy was there. I knew he was my best friend. His hair was a little bit longer than I remembered. That was odd. Sitting next to Tommy was...he was familiar, but I couldn't quite place him. The man started to get up.

"No, Dad, I'll do it." Tommy jumped up from his seat.

Dad? Oh yeah, that's who that was. Tommy's father. I hadn't come across him my previous life. But I had memories of him. He was around while I was growing up. Of course he would be. He was good friends with my parents. That's how I knew Tommy.

"You're shaking," Tommy noted when he took my hand. "Come on."

He led me out of the dining room and into the family room that overlooked the backyard and swimming pool. The moment we left the dining room, I could hear the voices of idle chatter floating all around us. It seemed as if no one gave me or Tommy a second thought.

He sat down on the couch and pulled me down on the cushion next to him. It made a whooshing sound as the air left it when I sat.

"That was quite a scene back there," he began. "What's the matter?"

Looking into his eyes, and being so close to him. There was a difference in his face. It had thinned out and I could see a few whiskers coming through.

"What?" he asked. "Why are you staring at me?"

"You look different," I told him. "Older somehow."

"We are the same age, 15. I don't think I look any different than..."

"Fifteen!" I interrupted. "What? That's not possible."

He narrowed his eyes at me. "Uh, yeah it is. You just had your birthday last week."

"I did? Oh."

It was all starting to come back to me. My last life. My questions. Two goons chasing Viv and me through the park into the forest. Our fight with said goons, and what must've been my death. I do remember Viv screaming right before I felt something hit me in the head and everything went black.

I must have died. Yeah, that had to be what happened. So how did I end up back here again? And at 15 years old? I literally aged two years in a matter of moments. But was that in the same life? Wait, no. It couldn't be. I could not have lost two years. And how could we have gotten out of the predicament in the cave? We didn't, that's how. I died. I just know it.

With a sharp intake of breath, something just came to me. What happened to Viv? I mean, yes, she's alive in this life, but what about that last life? Did they kill her? Did they let her go? I have to assume they killed her. With that, tears started running down my face. That poor girl. This is all my fault. How can I live with that?

Tommy and I both turned toward the dining room when raucous laughter poured in from that room. It was Beverly's voice that I recognized. She was enjoying her conversation that evening. I shook my head in disbelief. How in the world could she, or anyone for that matter, be enjoying themselves after what just happened a few moments ago in the dining room? I kind of freaked out and almost passed out, and no one seem to be bothered by it at all. What was wrong with those people?

"Yeah, you don't remember your own birthday?" Tommy's eyes narrowed, as if he really expected me to answer that question.

How to cover up the whole gamut of feelings surging through me at that point?

"Of course I remember my birthday. I'm just not feeling very good right now," I managed to choke out. "Would you mind getting me a glass of water?" It was the second time in only a few days, and two lives, that I had asked him to do that for me.

Without responding, Tommy jumped up and headed for the kitchen.

I leaned back on the couch to contemplate the predicament I had found myself in. Once again. Who in the world were those two men who stalked and attacked Viv and me? That really was my number one question to answer.

And what about Ivy, my real mother? I never even got the chance to go see her. I would have to make a point of doing that this time. If I could manage it before someone killed me, that is.

Once Tommy and his father left, and everything was cleaned up, I went up to bed. I just needed to get away from everyone and think about things. I must have been really tired, because the next thing I knew, warm sunshine was touching the side of my face and my eyelids. It woke me instantly.

Sitting up on my bed, it took me several seconds to realize what was going on and where I was. My shoulders slumped in response. I was exactly where I was hoping not to be. In a new life, with this new family that I didn't want, trying to figure out how to get back to my other family. And... trying not to get killed in the process.

"Girls! Breakfast is ready!" Beverly called from the kitchen.

Stan was nowhere to be seen, which was fine. I wanted to talk to Beverly, without both of them ganging up on me. I sat down in an empty chair. Beverly was just pulling pancakes from the pan.

"Bever...um, Mom," I corrected, "can you tell me about my adoption?" I was desperately hoping that she wouldn't freak out on me.

She turned from the stove and glared at me. "Honestly, Georgie, this again?"

Obviously we had already had some conversation about it. In my last lifetime, they were shocked that I found out. That was not the case this time. I wondered what we talked about. I had no memory of a conversation with them about this topic at all.

"So...we talked about this already?" I knew the question would probably sound really stupid to them. But somehow I needed to find out what had previously been said.

"Georgie, are you feeling all right? You know we talked about this." Beverly sounded more annoyed than concerned about me. "Honestly, I don't know how you forgot that." She slid two pancakes onto a plate and set it down on the table in front of Viv. "Yours are almost ready, Georgie."

"Oh yeah, of course." I tried my best to cover the fact that I didn't remember anything. "I guess it's too early in the morning for me."

It wasn't lost on me that Viv was sitting completely silent and listening to our whole exchange. She did have a mouth full of pancakes though.

"So, Georgie, why are you asking this again? I really want to know. And I do have a question for you. How did you even find out you were adopted? You never told us before. You just kind of left the whole thing hanging."

She set a plate of pancakes on the table in front of me and stood watching me, in anticipation of my answer.

Aw crap. How in the world was I going to answer that question? This must have happened before I showed up in this life. The last time I found out I was adopted, was when I ran into Harper at the mall. She's the one who told me everything. But I had no idea if I had met Harper in this lifetime. I would hate to bring all of that up and find out Harper never told me anything. I probably sat there for a full two minutes not saying a thing. That had to be very odd to see. But Beverly just watched me.

Finally just as I was about to say something like, 'Does it really matter?' which wasn't going to win me any daughter points, Viv jumped in.

"Oh, I'll tell her." Viv said with a flick of her wrist. She looked over at me and smiled. She very well knew that she was saving my butt.

I had a feeling that I was going to owe her.

Beverly looked over at her youngest child. "And what do you know about it, missy?"

"Well...I know that Georgie was snooping around and found her adoption papers." Viv smiled. It was a secret sort of smile, that told me she kind of liked throwing me under the bus.

Beverly turned back to me with raised eyebrows. "Is that right? You were snooping in my things?"

I shrugged.

"That's all you've got to say?" Beverly asked.

"Sorry?" I replied.

"Is that an apology, or a question? It sounds a lot like a question. Which is not an apology of any sort." Beverly admonished.

"Oh, sorry. I mean, yeah, I'm really sorry." The words were not coming out the way I intended them to.

Beverly shook her head. "Young lady, I don't even know what to do with you. What is it exactly that you would like to know about your adoption?"

"Well, okay, here goes. If I was kidnapped, then how come you were able to adopt me?" I blurted out.

Beverly dropped the spatula she had been tightly holding onto. We all looked at it when it landed with a clickity clack on the tile floor.

CHAPTER 2

After bending over to pick up the spatula that Beverly had just dropped in response to my bluntness about my kidnapping, she straightened up and narrowed her eyes at me.

"What in the world are you talking about?" Beverly walked over to the sink and dropped the spatula in it, which clanked around for a moment before coming to a silent halt. Turning back to face me, "You were not kidnapped. Where did you get a crazy idea like that?"

I glanced over at Viv, who had stopped chewing mid chew, and had her mouth hanging open, revealing its contents.

"Honestly Viv, close your mouth." I couldn't help the sarcasm in my voice.

She continued chewing as if everything was perfectly normal, which it wasn't at all.

"Georgie," Beverly interrupted. "Are you going to answer my question?"

I turned back toward her. "Oh, sorry. Um...someone told me I was kidnapped."

I was hoping that she wouldn't ask me who that someone was.

"Who told you that?" she sneered

Oops, that didn't take long.

"I'd rather not say." My eyes were turned downward, staring at the uneaten pancakes on my plate.

"That's not good enough, Georgie. You need to tell me who." Her voice had an edge to it. If she wasn't already irritated with my line of questioning, she certainly was now.

"It was my biological sister, that's who." I knew there would be follow up questions.

"What biological sister? The only sister you have is Viv." Beverly sat down in the chair across from me to continue her questioning.

I shook my head. "No, that's not true."

"Really?" Only her left eyebrow raised. The look on her face was one of suspicion. "You actually have another sister out there? I guess it's not out of the realm of possibility. But it's really true?"

I nodded. "It's really true."

What she didn't know was that yes, I had talked to Harper about being kidnapped. But it wasn't in this lifetime. Harper had no idea where I was at this point. I had to figure out what to do about that.

"And when did you talk to this sister of yours? And Where?" Beverly asked. There was still some trace in her voice that sounded as if she didn't believe a word I said.

"Oh I, um, I ran into her at the mall one day. She recognized me." Not technically a lie. It did happen, just not in this lifetime.

"How did she recognize you? I mean, it has been at least 12 years since she saw you last," Beverly asked.

"Yeah, I know. But somehow she did. She wasn't positive at first. But after we talked, we knew it was all true. And my name wasn't even changed when I was adopted. She called me Georgie."

"Well, that part is true. You were so young, and coming in to live with complete strangers, we didn't want to confuse you more by changing your name. We figured there was no way you would remember your previous family anyway. The adoption agency told us that your mother was a drug addict and abandoned you. Why does your sister, if that's who she really is, think that you were kidnapped?"

I let out a slow breath as I thought about how to answer. How do you tell your mother that something she has always thought to be true, was a complete lie? She had been deceived. And as a result, I had been taken from a family that loved me.

"Ivy was not a drug addict. And she definitely did not abandon me."

"Ivy? That's your mother's name?" Beverly asked. "What else did this girl tell you?"

"Yes, Ivy. Harper told me that I was taken from a family picnic when I was three years old. And I know it's the truth, because I remember it. Or at least part of it. I was lured to a car by a really tall man…"

My voice trailed off as an image flashed in my mind. A tall man, holding my hand and opening the car door for me.

"Oh my god, it was the same man!" I half yelled.

"What man?" Beverly reached over and patted me on the arm.

"The man that chased Viv and me into a cave and k…" Oops, I couldn't say he killed me. That would make no sense to them. "He…he…oh, I don't really remember after that."

"Nobody chased us into a cave," Viv finally chimed in, with a bit of incredulity to her voice. "What are you talking about?"

There was a confused look on her face, and rightly so. Of course she wouldn't remember that at all. It happened in my last lifetime. I still don't know if she was killed that day. That's something I will never be able to find out. I'll just have to live with the fact that she probably did die. And it was all because of me.

That made me wonder about something. Did the world go on once I was killed? If it did, then that must mean that lifetime is still running, concurrently with the one I'm in. I don't even know how that is possible. The whole idea of it all made my head hurt.

I needed to come up with a plausible explanation of what I had just told Beverly. Something that would placate Viv.

I turned to my little sister. "Oh, you're right. I guess you weren't there. It was just me. Sorry, I was confused."

The only response I got from Viv was a pinched expression. She was 12. What else was I to expect?

"What man was chasing you through the forest and into a cave?" Beverly's voice was rising and rising. She was on the verge of crying at my declaration. Her eyes were filling with tears.

How was I going to explain what I just said? Of course my mother would be horrified at the thought of me being chased by some stranger into a cave.

"Are you seriously saying that the man who kidnapped you originally, if that's what really happened, recently chased you through the forest?" Beverly added. "What happened next?"

She looked like she was barely breathing, holding her breath in anticipation of my answer.

"Oh, well...nothing happened," I lied. "I hid from him and when he couldn't find me, he left, I guess." I shrugged one shoulder, hoping that would placate her. I was pretty sure it wouldn't.

Having eaten no more than a bite or two, I pushed my plate away from me. "I'm not really hungry."

Beverly glared at me. She didn't like my answer at all. It was pretty vague, so who could blame her?

I made a decision right there and then, and I planned on carrying it through. I would go see Ivy. I was terrified at the thought, but it was something I needed to do.

CHAPTER 3

It didn't take me long to do some research online and find my mother. Her name was Ivy Wells. That much I knew for sure. There were several stories about my kidnapping. That was proof to me. I knew it was me, especially after my conversation with Harper.

On the bus over to Red Lake, I had no choice but to sit next to a man who smelled of garlic and whiskey. He said hello to me as I sat down, and ignored me the rest of the ride. He had a book he was reading, which was way more interesting than I was. Not that I wanted to have a conversation with a total stranger anyway. I wanted to take the time to contemplate how I was going to approach Ivy and what I was going to say.

The bus deposited me only a few blocks away from Ivy's house. Though I had taken some time to think about it, I suddenly began shaking at the thought of facing my mother. The woman who had suffered through having her daughter kidnapped and had no idea whatever happened to her. Would she even know me? Would she believe that I was the person I said I was? I was hoping that Harper was there. Even though we had not spoken in this lifetime, she clearly would recognize me, like she did last time. At least I was hoping that was the case.

Ivy's neighborhood was a nice middle class place. The houses were all lined up in a nice straight line, on a nice straight street. All of them were neutral colors with white trim. Every lawn was manicured perfectly. Not a single car up on blocks. The area seemed vaguely familiar. But then again, I was only three years old when I was taken. I probably hadn't spent a lot of time outside wandering the neighborhood.

Coming upon the correct address, I stopped to contemplate before I dared walk up to the door. Should I just walk up and knock on the door like a normal person? What else would I do? Afraid that the neighbors might become suspicious of someone just standing out on the sidewalk staring at a house, I decided I needed to get on with it.

My feet seemed to barely move as I approached the house. My body shook, as if it was freezing outside, but it was summertime. I knew it was just nerves. At least I had a speech prepared. I didn't want to get up to the door and start mumbling over my words. I willed my arm to rise and knock on the door. It was a soft knock. I half hoped no one would hear it and I could leave without them ever knowing I had been there.

Just as I turned to leave, the door flew open. I spun around and came face-to-face with Ivy Wells.

I recognized her. That face was in my dreams. That red, curly hair of hers. I would know it anywhere. I knew in that instant that none of this was a mistake. I was definitely her daughter and I belonged there.

The experience of seeing her for the first time almost knocked the wind out of me. I started breathing heavily and for a moment I couldn't catch my breath. When my vision started going dark, I reached around for something to hang onto. I was going to fall, that was inevitable. There was a bench seat sitting on the porch just to the left of the door. My hand found it and steadied me.

I must have looked a sight, because Ivy came out onto the patio. She reached over and patted me on the shoulder.

"Are you all right?" she asked me. I could hear the concern in her voice. I was pretty sure she hadn't recognized me. "Here, why don't you sit down." She gestured toward the bench I was currently hanging onto for dear life.

"Oh, okay," I managed to choke out as I sat down.

It took everything I had in me to look up at her. I didn't know what to do. I didn't know what to say. I mean, what do you say to a mother you have not seen in 12 years? My prepared speech was out the window.

Our eyes locked and Ivy gasped.

"You...you look...just like my...oh it couldn't be." It was all she could do to get a sentence out.

I was her daughter. I wanted her to say it. I needed her to say it.

Ivy sat down on the bench next to me. I think she needed to catch her breath also. She turned and looked me in the eyes once more.

"Are you...I mean, is it possible that you are..." She just couldn't get the words out.

"Your daughter," I offered. "Are you asking if I'm your daughter?"

She nodded, without speaking. I think I left the poor woman speechless.

"Yes, I believe I am," I told her.

"Oh my god." Ivy burst out crying and bent over with her face in her hands. She stayed like that for at least a full minute before coming up for air.

I felt a little uncomfortable, not quite knowing what to do in the situation I had found myself in. Do I put my arm around her and comfort her? She was my mother after all. But she was also a stranger. She might think it was odd if I did that. So, I just sat there and let her cry. We had plenty of time to talk.

Before I realized what was happening, she leaned over and wrapped her arms around me. "Oh, Georgie, I can't believe you are here!" she wailed.

I let her hug me and I hugged her back. I didn't plan to cry. I didn't expect to cry. But I did cry nevertheless. I couldn't help it. Here I was, with my mother once again.

After several minutes, her sobs finally subsided and she released me. Leaning back to get a better look at me, she wiped her eyes with the back of her hand.

"I can't believe this. I'm such a blubbering mess," she told me. "I finally have my baby girl back here with me and all I can do is slobber all over her." She smiled at her own words.

I shook my head slightly. "No, it's okay. I totally understand."

"I should probably start by asking you what your name is."

"It's Georgie. My adoptive parents didn't want to confuse me by changing my name," I explained.

Her eyebrows lifted in response. "Your adoptive parents? You mean the people who kidnapped you? Who are they? I need to know." Her voice turned angry in an instant.

Putting my palms up in front of me, I knew that I needed to put a stop to that thinking right away. "No, they didn't kidnap me. Someone else did," I tried to explain. "In fact, they didn't even know I was kidnapped until I told them recently."

"Reeeeally." She drawled out the word in an exaggerated tone. She didn't believe me.

"Yes, really." My voice sounded defensive. But I couldn't help it. "You know, I've changed so much since you saw me last. How did you even recognize me? I mean, I was only three years old." I was doing my best to change the subject.

"Oh…well…you aren't going to believe this, but I'm going to say it anyway." Her voice was apprehensive.

"After all I've gone through, I doubt you could say anything to me that I wouldn't believe," I told her truthfully.

"I saw you grow up in another life. That's how I recognized you." She drew in a quick breath and held it, in anticipation of my response.

My eyebrows shot up. "Really? Wow that's just...just..." I had no words.

"Crazy?" she offered. "Completely and utterly insane?"

"Actually, no. I know I've lived other lives. I just didn't know you had," I explained.

"You have?" she asked. She then looked off into the distance as if contemplating something deep. "I don't know why I'm really surprised. It definitely runs in the family." She laughed for just a moment. "I call it the family curse."

"It runs in the family?" I was shocked. "I had no idea. I thought I was the only one on the planet this happens to."

"No, you definitely are not. Hey," she stood, "why don't you come inside? I'll get you something to drink and we can talk some more. What do you say?"

I nodded and followed her inside.

Once seated and with a cola in front of me at the kitchen bar, we began talking.

Ivy leaned over the other side of the bar. She was standing in the kitchen. "You know, I've thought about you every single day for the past 12 years."

I nodded, stifling tears that wanted to spill over.

"Tell me where you've been living, and the people who raised you."

I spent the next several minutes telling her all about Beverly and Stan, and my little sister Viv. I did not give out their names. I wasn't sure if that was a good idea or not, having been kidnapped and all. I did mention Viv's name, but that was the only one. I also told Ivy that I had only been in this lifetime for a very short while. Days only.

"How did you, you know...die? Is that too much for you to think about right now?" Ivy asked.

"No, it's okay. I've thought about it a lot. I'm not actually 100 percent sure how I died, but I think my head was bashed in." It was weird saying it out loud.

"Oh honey, I understand," Ivy replied. "I've been stabbed, strangled, fallen into the sinkhole. You name it." She stifled a laugh. "I've made my peace with it."

My eyes went wide. "The sinkhole? I'm pretty sure I died there too."

"Oh no. It's horrible, isn't it?" Ivy asked.

I just nodded. What else was there to say?

"You know," I began, "I said that my new family had nothing to do with my kidnapping, but I'm not sure that's entirely true."

"Really? Why do you say that?" Ivy didn't believe they were innocent either. I think she was just humoring me.

"Because the person that killed me this last time, you know the smashed head incident? Well he was the same person who kidnapped me. At least I'm pretty sure he was the same person. Remember, I was three. I have some memories of that time, but not a lot. I do remember getting into a car with the man, but I can't be positive that it was the same time I was kidnapped." I said it all so fast, that I was hoping Ivy was keeping up with my ramblings. "Even if it wasn't the same time, I know it was the same man. So that tells me that the family knows him. I guess it doesn't prove they had anything to do with it though."

Ivy put her hand over mine on the counter. It was a loving gesture. "It's all right, Georgie. I get it."

"Georgie," a voice behind me said. "Mom, did you say Georgie?"

We both looked up to find Harper and an older boy standing next to her. They both looked to be in their early twenties.

"Oh, Harper, Jack. I found your sister!" Ivy exclaimed. "Or rather, she found me."

CHAPTER 4

With Harper and Jack having just walked in on Ivy and me talk-ing, Ivy told them she had just found me. All three sets of eyes were planted firmly on me. I felt the heat creep into my cheeks.

"I don't believe this. This is really her? Our Georgie?" Jack stared at me without blinking.

Ivy nodded. "Yeah, it's really her. I'm positive."

No one else spoke for what seemed like the longest time. Jack was the first one to break the silence. He was also the first one to walk over and hug me. I began crying, causing him to pull out of my embrace and look me in the eyes.

"Oh Georgie, I'm sorry that I made you cry." His right hand brushed some wet strands of hair from my cheek. "I'm your big brother. You know that, right?"

I nodded. "I...yeah...I figured that out," I told him with a smile.

Harper and Ivy joined in, causing one big group hug. It was all so overwhelming to me.

Once everyone found their spot around the kitchen, and I had composed myself, I was peppered with questions. Where had I been? Who was I living with? Did I know who my kidnapper was? I answered all of their questions to the best of my ability. They also told me all about their lives, how it all had been without me being there. They told me of the day I was kidnapped, the subsequent investigation, and the fact that no one could ever find a trace of me. They weren't sure I was even alive.

That last part hurt me most of all. My family, the ones who loved me the most, were tortured with the thought of me being dead all these years. And here I was, alive and well, living with another family. Loving another family. And having no idea that Ivy and her children existed until just recently.

They also explained to me that my father had passed away a few years prior. I wasn't quite comfortable enough with them to ask for details. I'm sure it was still tough on them to talk about it. I figured I would get the story at another time.

Inevitably, the subject of reliving our lives came up. Ivy told us about her reliving her lives. She even told us about two different children that she had in her first life, that don't exist now. That was hard to hear. I can't even imagine living through something like that. She loved those two children and now she will never see them again.

Then Jack regaled us with stories about him reliving his lives. Apparently he had been convicted of murdering some boys and spent 20 years in prison. Then he was executed and came back in a new life. That was a crazy story. I was so glad to know that story was not going to happen again. At least I hoped not. The truth was that I had no idea what was going to happen or not. We might do all of this over and over again, a hundred times.

"You know," I began with my own story, "I drowned in Red Lake when I was seven years old. I know none of you remember that, of course. But it happened." All eyes were wide. "Then when I came back, I was five years old. I didn't realize it at the time, of course, but I obviously came back in another life."

"Are you serious?" Harper asked, her mouth hanging half open.

I nodded. "Yes. I told Ivy about it at the time, in my first life, I think. But I'm pretty sure that she didn't believed me."

I glanced over at Ivy to gauge her reaction.

She shook her head. "No, honey, I don't remember that at all. But if you say it happened, I have no doubt that it did. You definitely inherited the family curse."

"I wonder why I didn't inherit it?" Harper asked. "As far as I know, this is my one and only life. Obviously I've lived others, because all of you remember me and your other lives. But I don't remember any of them. I just wonder why?"

Ivy put her arm around Harper's shoulders. "That is the million dollar question. As far as I know, no one has been able to figure out why this happens."

"Is there anyone else in the family that this has happened to? Or are we the only lucky ones?" I asked.

"Oh, I almost forgot," Ivy jumped in. "My grandfather, Sam, relived his lives. His were a little different than ours. I'll have to tell you that story another time."

I nodded, not wanting to push. I knew I would hear all about it later.

"I need to tell you something," Jack said directly to me. Then he looked around at our mother and sister. "I need to tell you all something, actually."

"What is it?" Ivy asked.

"I don't remember the date, but maybe about two months before you disappeared," he said to me directly, "we were all at the park and I remember seeing someone try to grab you. You started crying. I heard you and started running toward you. That's when the man saw me and ran in the other direction. I didn't get a very good look at him, but I'm sure that I didn't recognize him."

Ivy gasped. "What? Why didn't you tell me this before?" Her words were part shock and part anger.

He shrugged. "I don't know. I was only about 12 at the time. I was afraid that you would be mad at me for not watching Georgie closer. Nothing actually happened. I just figured the man was trying to talk to her. It didn't really dawn on me at the time that maybe he was attempting a kidnapping. Of course, later, when she really was kidnapped, I thought about the man. But I didn't get a good look at him, so I decided not to say anything."

Ivy looked away. I think she was having trouble meeting her son's gaze. She probably just needed time to process what she had just heard. I figured it might be the perfect time to change the subject. Harper must have had the same idea as I did, because before I could say anything, she jumped in.

"Are you moving in with us now?" Harper asked me directly.

I was taken off guard by that question. It had never even occurred to me that I could just move in with them. I was still 15 after all, and the Taylor family were my legal guardians, I guess. I still wasn't entirely sure that my adoption was illegal.

"Oh, uh, I don't know," I answered truthfully. "This just happened to me. This life, I mean. I'm not really sure what I should be doing."

"Harper's right," Ivy jumped in. "You should move in with us right away. Those people kidnapped you and you can't stay with them."

"But I'm not sure that they did," I told them. "It's entirely possible that they just wanted to adopt a child and I was the one available. They may not know anything about it."

"You don't actually believe that, do you?" Harper asked, her lips pursed.

I shrugged. "I don't know. I guess anything's possible. I mean, look at this family? We relive our lives. That's freaking insane, when you think about it."

Everyone just nodded. They knew it was crazy, and they couldn't deny it.

"I'm really hoping that you all can help me find some answers to all of this," I told them. "You've already been a big help."

"We want to help you," Jack told me. "We just don't know where to start. I know you were kidnapped. It was never solved by the cops, so how can we solve it?"

"Maybe you can ask your other family what they know." Harper put both hands up and made air quotes around the word 'family.'

"I've tried. They claim they don't know anything. I don't know if there's anyone in the family that I can trust. Except my sister, Viv. But she's only 12 and doesn't know anything. The family told me they just adopted me and that's all they know."

"Then how about the adoption agency?" Jack offered.

"But how would the adoption agency have gotten her in the first place?" Harper asked. "Doesn't someone have to give her up for adoption first?"

"Hmm," Ivy jumped in. "That's a good question." She looked over our heads, deep in thought. Meeting my eyes again, she continued. "Maybe someone pretended to be your parent and gave you up for adoption."

"But why would they take me in the first place if they were just going to give me up?" I asked. It didn't make any sense to me.

Ivy gasped and we all turned to her. "This could all be part of a crooked adoption ring. You know, black market babies."

She looked to each of us for a reaction. I'm sure we were all a mixture of confusion and shock. I was still very young and didn't really know much, if anything at all, about black market babies. I had a feeling I was about to find out a lot more on the subject.

"Soooo...wait...are you saying that someone kidnapped me

by the lake that day, just to sell me to someone? My parents…I mean my adoptive parents, are well off. You think they bought me?" My head was reeling with all the possibilities. "Is that what you mean?"

Ivy took a deep breath. "Maybe. Or just maybe they knew nothing, and were just victims in this whole thing, like you were. None of us know anything at this point."

"I don't know what to do," I told them honestly. "I don't know where I belong. I have memories of growing up with them, but also memories of you guys. Until I was seven at least. You know, the time I drowned in Red Lake? I know you don't remember, but I do. I have no other memories past that age. So I don't think I ever lived with you past the age of seven."

"You're probably right about your memories, honey." Ivy put her hand up on my shoulder. It was a comforting gesture. "But you did grow up with us, at least once that I remember. So, I do know the answer to where you belong. It's right here with us."

I nodded. "You are right, of course. But I think I should at least go back temporarily. I need to find some answers. I can't do that from here."

The look on Ivy's face just broke my heart. "It could be dangerous, Georgie."

"It won't be for long, I promise. And I'm in no danger. I've lived with them most of my life…" I looked over at Ivy. I could tell that my comment made her heart sink. Who could blame her? "But none of that matters. You are my mom, and always will be. One thing I really need to do is check on my little sister, Viv. I'm worried about her. She's innocent in all of this, and I want to make sure she's all right. Can you understand that?"

Ivy nodded. She was stifling back tears. "You know, I do understand. But, I just can't let you go. Even if the people who raised you are not connected to your kidnapping, someone they know might be. If they get wind that you are suspicious and asking questions, it can be dangerous whether you think so or not. Believe me when I say that I've been in many dangerous situations. Many. And it's difficult to get out once you are there." She reached for my hand. "Georgie, please stay here. Let me call the police and have them investigate this. It's the sane and safest thing to do."

I nodded, without actually answering her.

"Come on, let's all go out on the back porch and sit. I'll make some tea and we can mull this over some more. Okay?" She was mostly asking me.

"Yeah, okay."

We all headed for the back door, when I stopped in my tracks. "I'll be out in just a minute. I need to make a phone call."

"All right, see you in a minute," Ivy called over her left shoulder.

The moment the door was shut, I bolted.

CHAPTER 5

God, I felt horrible for taking off from Ivy's house. But what choice did I really have? I had to get back to my other family, and I needed to find answers. I wasn't going to find them staying at Ivy's house. She meant well, of course. And she was my mother. She had all the rights in the world to expect me to stay. Calling the police and having them investigate was probably the smart way to go. And probably the safest way to go. But I had no way of knowing if the police would take all of this seriously and do their best to find out what was going on. I had no idea who was involved. I needed to find out on my own what happened. Besides, I didn't know how much longer I would be in this lifetime.

And then there was the most important thing back at that house. Viv. I couldn't just leave her with those people. They seemed nice enough and I remembered them being a loving family. But who knows what could happen to her if I disappeared and left her alone with them. They might consort with some unsavory people. I just couldn't let that happen.

Once I was safely out the door and on my way back to my

adoptive family, I called Ivy. She had given me her phone number to use anytime I wanted, and I felt this was a good time.

She didn't know who my adoptive family was. I hadn't told any of them. I'm not sure if that was smart of me or not. They would have no way of finding me if something went wrong. Suddenly I was regretting that decision. Someone should know where I was. You know, just in case.

"Hello? Georgie? Where are you?" The panic in Ivy's voice shown through.

"I just called to tell you that I'm all right. And that I'm sorry. It's just important to me that I find out what's going on. And I need to make sure that Viv is going to be okay. I hope you can understand that. I promise that I will come back to you. Please don't call the sheriff yet," I begged.

There was a long pause in the other end of the line.

"Ivy?" I wasn't sure if I should call her 'mom' yet, so I stuck with 'Ivy' for the time being. I hoped she understood why. This was all just so new to me. I had two mothers, technically. One who adopted and raised me, and another who I was stolen from at such a young age. The whole thing just tore me apart.

"Yes, I'm here." Her voice was meek. I heard shuddering breaths through the phone line and knew that she was trying to shield her disappointment, or her heartbreak, from me. It wasn't working.

"I'm sorry. Truly I am," I told her. "I just need to do this. I'll call you back soon, okay?"

"I guess I don't have much choice, do I? Especially since I don't know where you are." Ivy's voice had changed from sadness to a bit of anger. "Are you going to tell me where you are?"

I shook my head. Then, realizing that she couldn't see me, "Not just yet, no. I'm sorry."

Ivy's voice softened. "You don't have to keep saying that you are sorry. I know. And I am too. Be safe, and please call me tomorrow?"

"I will." I hung up the phone without another word. I feared that she would weasel my whereabouts out of me if I stayed on the line any longer.

"Well, that's done. For now," I said out loud, to no one at all.

~

I walked in to find Viv lying on the living room couch, watching TV. She barely looked up at me as I entered the room.

"Where are Stan and Bev...um, I mean Mom and Dad?" I asked her.

Viv gave me the side eye, but she didn't respond to the fact that I had just called them by their first names. She was too engrossed in whatever it is she was watching, and very unconcerned about me by the looks of it.

"They went to Aunt Eve's house. You know that," Viv said without removing her eyes from the TV.

"And they just left you here all alone?"

"I'm 12 and can take care of myself. Besides, I'm not alone. You're here." Her voice was flippant.

"How come no one told me?" I asked.

That time she turned her head to face me full on. She still didn't budge an inch from her comfortable spot on the couch. "What are you talking about? They have been planning this trip for weeks. Months maybe. You know all about it."

Yeah, maybe I did, and just didn't realize it. Since I had only been in this current life a few days.

I shrugged. "Oh, I forgot."

It was clear to me that Viv was going to be no help whatsoever. So, while she stayed in front of that TV, I decided to do a little detective work myself.

The most obvious place to start, in my mind anyway, was my

parents' bedroom. Wasn't that where most parents kept all their most secret papers? Stuff they didn't want their children to see? At least I hoped that was the case.

I looked over my shoulder just as I left the living room, to make sure Viv wasn't following me. She was paying no attention whatsoever to my movements. So, I moved on. Upon entering my parents bedroom, I went straight for their dresser. It seemed the most obvious place to stash paperwork. Kids were not usually allowed to get into their parents' dresser. It was a sacred place for parents to keep their underwear and stuff. Why paperwork usually got stuffed in the underwear drawer, was beyond me. Maybe they figured the kids didn't want to be touching their parents' unmentionables.

I did find some paperwork after about ten minutes of searching. It wasn't in their dresser, but it was in a box at the top of their closet shelf. There were some legal papers in there, but I couldn't find anything that had anything to do with me. An interesting thing I did find though, were some legal papers with Tommy's dad's name on them. I had forgotten that he was an attorney. The paperwork was just about their home purchase. So nothing to do with me at all.

A few more minutes of searching yielded no results. I left the bedroom and went to my room to try to figure out my next steps. I thought about going to see Tommy's father, Trent. He was the family attorney and perhaps had some knowledge of my adoption. Or at least maybe he could point me in the right direction.

I called Ivy to get her take on the idea of seeing Trent.

"I think it's a good idea," she told me. "Since he's your... their...family attorney, he's got to know something."

Her changing words in the middle of her sentence didn't escape my notice.

"I will then," I told her. "It's late now, but I can go in the morning."

CHAPTER 6

The next morning, I looked up Trent's office address and showed up at 9am sharp. I found him standing in the lobby, speaking with a pretty young woman in very tall high heels. He was handing her some documents, and speaking softly to her. He smiled when he noticed me walk up. The young woman looked at me from head to toe, with no expression whatsoever, turned and headed toward the elevators.

Trent walked over, standing next to me, and put his arm around my shoulders, giving me a friendly squeeze. It was a nice, brotherly type of gesture.

"Georgie, so what do I owe the pleasure of your visit today?"

"I um, well, I wanted to talk to you about something? Is that okay?" I felt a bit awkward, because even though he was a family friend, I felt like I barely knew him. But I did have memories of him while growing up, so he had definitely been around.

"Sure, of course. For you, anything," he said with a smile. "Come on, we can talk in my office." I followed dutifully.

Once we were both seated, him in his large chair, and me directly across the desk from him, he spoke first.

"So what can I do for you?" he asked. He was giving me his

undivided attention, something I didn't expect from a busy attorney like him.

"Well," I began, "you are going to think this is strange of me to come to you for advice, but I want to know more about my kidnapping and adoption." I figured there was no better way than to rip the bandage right off. I bit my lower lip.

His eyebrows shot up. "Your what? Did you say kidnapping?" He knew that's exactly what I had just said.

I nodded.

"Georgie, you weren't kidnapped. You were just adopted. Plain and simple. What gives you the idea that you were kidnapped?"

"My mother told me I was," I answered.

"Why would Beverly say that? I'm sure she doesn't think that. I'm confused," he replied.

"Not Beverly. My mother. My actual mother. Ivy Wells."

Now I'm not absolutely positive, but I could swear that I saw him stifle a gasp.

"Who? I don't know that name. Where did you hear that name?"

"I told you, I talked to her. She is the one that said I was kidnapped," I tried to explain. I was beginning to feel like he wasn't actually listening to what I was trying to tell him.

"Honey, I don't really know much about where you came from. But I'm sure you weren't kidnapped. Your parents would not have been able to adopt you if that were the case."

"I may have been part of a black market baby ring." I had done some online research into the topic. I knew way more than anyone my age should know about it.

"A what? Where did you hear that term?"

"The internet. You've heard of it right?" I smiled. He did not reciprocate.

"You really have to stop believing all the crazy stuff you read on the internet. Yes, black market baby rings exist, but you weren't part of one. You were just given up by your mother and adopted to Beverly and Stan. End of story."

I couldn't let that one go. "No, not end of story. I know for a fact that I was kidnapped. I just need some help finding out who did it and why. Like, if I was part of the black market baby ring, then why was I adopted? Don't those people usually charge a lot of money for babies? I'm sure that Beverly and Stan didn't pay any money for me. At least as far as I know they didn't. They told me they didn't know anything about a kidnapping and just adopted me as usual."

Whew, I needed to take a breath after all of that. I had barely had a chance to breathe, because I was trying to say it so fast. I didn't want Trent to interrupt me and tell me how wrong I was. I wanted him to hear the whole story. At least the part I knew anyway. I stood up and walked around the office a bit. The chair felt much too confining.

"It seems as if you already have your mind made up about what happened," he started. "So why come to me?"

"Because you are an attorney. Maybe you can help me find some answers. What kind of attorney are you anyway?" I looked around his brown office, as if there was going to be a neon sign flashing above his head. "You're not a divorce lawyer are you? I don't think that would be very useful." I smiled again. He gave me a tiny one sided curl of his lips. Trying to humor me, I guess.

"No, I'm not a divorce lawyer. I'm an adoption attorney."

Then it was my turn to gasp. "What? Why didn't you tell me that?"

"You didn't ask." He leaned back in his chair and crossed his arms in front of him.

"Are you...did you...I..." I couldn't get the words out.

Trent leaned forward in his chair, groaning at the effort it took for him to do so. "Georgie are you all right?" He patted the air in front of him. "Just calm down. Take a deep breath and then try to tell me again what you are trying to say."

I took a moment to get my breathing back to normal. I wondered what the chances were that my parents' close family friend was an attorney and that he had absolutely nothing to do with my adoption.

Before I had a chance to speak, Trent put his hand up in the air in a stopping sort of motion. "I know what you are going to ask. And no, I had nothing to do with your adoption."

"Oh." It was all I could manage to say. I stared at my feet.

"I suppose you are going to say that Viv was kidnapped also? Since that seems to be the theme right now," Trent said, with a flippant tone.

My eyes shot up to meet his. "Viv? What? Are you saying that she was adopted too?"

His eyes widened. It was obvious to me at that point that he had said something he shouldn't have. "Oh Georgie, I'm sorry. I thought you knew that she was also adopted. Damn, I have a big mouth."

I shook my head slightly. "No, I had no idea." I stood up and walked around the room. I couldn't sit still for one more moment. "How could you all not tell me? And more importantly, how could you not tell Viv? She has no clue that she was adopted."

"The honest truth is that I thought you both knew. Stanley told me years ago that they were going to tell you when you were old enough to understand. I just didn't realize that hadn't happened yet." He sounded sincere.

"Did you do Viv's adoption? Where did she come from? Who are her parents? What..."

"Whoa, hold on a minute." This time he put both hands up in the air between us.

I stopped short and turned to face him.

"I think you need to go home and have a talk with your parents. Look, I'm sure both yours and Viv's adoptions were completely legitimate."

"Then how do you explain that I was kidnapped and then put up for adoption? I saw the kidnapping articles online. They looked for me for a long time." I was trying the best I could to keep the anger from my voice.

"I think that woman is confused. Sure, maybe she did have a child kidnapped. But where is the proof that the child is you? She might just be a lonely woman looking for someone to grasp onto. You are probably about the right age, and maybe even look a little bit like her. So you were the perfect person for her to project all of her loneliness and anger onto."

"No, you don't understand. I remember her. I know for a fact that she is my biological mother," I explained.

"You were only three years old. How can you possibly remember her?" It was a legitimate question.

There was no way I could tell him that I lived with Ivy in another lifetime, and that I was a little bit older. Somehow, I needed to convince him that even though I was only three, I did remember her.

"Um, I just do. I don't know." Yeah, that sounded legit. I sat back down and squirmed in my seat.

"Georgie, you were so young. Kids that young are really impressionable. You might remember someone like her. Or you may have even heard someone talk about her, and now thinks she's the one. But I promise you, she isn't. Or..." he looked above my head, deep in thought, "she probably isn't. I guess I can't say that for a fact. But you weren't kidnapped. So the chances of her being your actual mother are minuscule at best."

He was wrong. I knew that. I remembered Ivy, though there was no way I could convince him of that. I couldn't convince him that a three-year-old definitely remembered her, all these years later. There was also the fact that Ivy remembered me growing up. In another lifetime, of course. She knew I was her long lost daughter. There was no doubt in her mind. I knew it also. I just didn't know how to prove it.

"Okay, obviously you don't believe me." I waved my hand up in the air in a dismissive manner. "That's fine, whatever. But even so, I was hoping you could help me with something."

"Sure, anything for you."

"Can you help me start an investigation with the sheriff?" I asked, holding my breath for an answer.

"How am I supposed to do that, when you weren't even kidnapped? Your adoption was on the up and up. I'm sure of it." He looked a little pale to me, but it could have been my imagination.

I ignored his statement. I was tired of trying to convince him of my story. He wasn't going to believe me, and I just had to accept that. "Please just help me? I would go to the sheriff directly, but they won't believe a 15 year old. You are a respected attorney," I assumed, "so they will listen to you."

He thought for a moment. "Yeah, okay. I'll talk to them as soon as I can. What is this woman's name that you believe is your biological mother?"

"Ivy Wells."

He picked up a pen and wrote down her name. "Okay, got it. I'll let you know how it goes." He stood up and walked me to his office door. That was my cue to leave.

CHAPTER 7

I was flying high after leaving Trent's office that day. I finally had someone who was going to help me in this whole crazy mess. I knew that Ivy would help me in a second, but the problem is that she didn't know anything. All she knew was that I had been kidnapped. If she had known anything, she would've done something about it along time ago.

I knew exactly where I would go next. To Beverly. My adoptive mother. I needed an ally in the family, and she was the obvious choice. Viv was too young to do anything to help me. Besides, she had been adopted also. And I had no idea what the circumstances were of her adoption. I would have to look into it at some point, but not right at the moment. I needed to deal with my own kidnapping and adoption first.

I found Beverly in the kitchen, making sandwiches for lunch.

She looked up as I walked in. "Oh Georgie, there you are. Where in the world have you been? I called some of your friends, but no one had seen you."

Her voice was more inquisitive than worried. Maybe it was normal for me to just leave the house and not tell anyone.

Though I have memories of living there, I wasn't sure about all of my behavior.

"I went to see Trent."

Beverly looked up from the turkey and cheese sandwich she was just about to cut in half. Her hand and knife hung just inches above the bread in some sort of weird frozen stance. She tilted her head as she looked at me. "Trent? Why would you go see him?"

"I wanted to talk to him about my adoption. And my kidnapping," I blurted out.

Her hand resumed its downward trajectory and cut the sandwich with perfect precision, before acknowledging what I had just said.

She took a deep breath and let out a huff. "Oh, that again?" She never looked at me while speaking, but continued with her lunch preparations.

"Bev...um, Mom," I corrected myself, "can we just sit over here and talk for a few minutes?" I gestured with my hand toward the family room. Viv was nowhere to be seen.

She looked at me, then toward the family room. "Georgie, I'm in the middle of making lunch."

"Please? It won't take long. No one will starve in the next ten minutes."

With a bit of an exasperated sigh, she pushed the plate with a sandwich on it to the side, picked up a napkin, wiped her hands thoroughly, and walked around the kitchen bar toward me. "Okay fine. But let's keep this quick, okay?"

I followed her into the family room. "Okay."

I spent the next several minutes telling her about my visit with Trent. I told her that I knew I was kidnapped, even if she wasn't aware of it, and that I knew that Ivy was my biological mother. Beverly wasn't buying any of it. I don't know why she felt so inclined to be against my story. She had no way of knowing what my life was like before they adopted me. She was told that my mother gave me up because she couldn't take care of me anymore. She was told that my mother was a drug addict. None of that was accurate.

After speaking with her, I was convinced that she was going to be of no help. She was convinced that my story was completely fabricated. At least I had Trent on my side. He was going to talk to the sheriff and help me investigate this whole thing. This meant that the wheels were starting to move, even if Beverly and Stan didn't want to help. I hadn't spoken directly with Stan about it, at least not recently, but Beverly told me that he believed the same things that she did.

Viv walked in, just at the end of our conversation. "Is lunch ready yet, Mom? I'm starving."

Beverly jumped off the couch, welcoming the interruption. She didn't really want to be talking with me about this. That was painfully obvious.

"Yes, it's just about ready, Viv. Give me a minute to get you something to drink." She turned to me. "Georgie, would you like a sandwich? I'm happy to make you one."

I shook my head. "No thank you. I think I'll go for a walk."

I headed straight for the front door. I walked down the road to the park and wandered around for a little while. Not a half hour after I arrived at the park, I climbed up on top of a park bench and sat on the table portion. I put my face into my hands, lamenting the situation I had found myself in. I didn't know what to do at that point. My parents were going to be no help. The only person I had any chance of getting some sort of help from, was Trent. And even then, I didn't know how long that was going to take. I wondered if he had already spoken with the sheriff. Though it had not been that long since I left his office, so I doubted he had already taken care of it. I figured I would wait a couple of days before I called him to see if anything was happening.

When I lifted my face up out of my hands, I caught a

glimpse of a man walking around, trying not to be noticed. He was staying near the tree line of the forest and glanced up at me.

My breath caught in my throat. It was the same man who had chased me and Viv into the forest in my previous life. It was that same tall, thin man that I am positive was the one who kidnapped me when I was three years old.

I didn't know what to do. I could barely breathe. He turned and caught my eye. When that happened, he knew that I recognized him. I could see it in his face. Without hesitation, he broke out into a dead run, straight at me.

In my effort to get off of the top of the picnic bench, my right foot got caught on the seating portion and I tumbled off, face first into the grass. I didn't have time to think about how my face was probably covered in grass and dirt, as well as my clothing. I flew up off the ground and took off in a sprint.

Though he was probably 20 years older than I was, he was faster. I glanced over my shoulder and he was gaining on me. I started to panic, not knowing which way to go. Because of this, I hesitated just long enough for him to catch up with me.

He grabbed a handful of my hair and yanked me back, flipping me up off my feet. I landed hard on my back, knocking the wind out of me. He knelt down beside me, hanging on. I struggled to get up, but I could barely breathe and he was holding tightly onto my hair.

Leaning over me, he bent down so that his face was only a couple of inches from my ear. He was so close that I could feel his hot breath on my ear. It made me cringe.

He whispered into my ear. "You need to back off, do you hear me? No more questions about being kidnapped. No more questions about your adoption. Do I make myself clear?" His words were slow and deliberate.

I shivered and nodded in response. I couldn't speak. No words would come out.

"Good. Because if I have to come back, I will kill your little sister. Got it?"

"Yeah...I...got it." I managed to choke the words out.

He abruptly released my hair and stood. He stayed there, watching me for at least another full minute. I dared not move. Then, just as quickly, he turned and walked away.

I laid there for probably three full minutes, before I could move a muscle. As I was lying there, I wondered why no one had interfered in our scuffle. I hadn't heard a single thing from anyone else. No excited chatter. No one running to help me. No children playing. Nothing.

When I finally sat up, I understood why. I was the only one in the park. My aggressor was long gone and not a single other person was anywhere to be seen. It was usually a busy place, so I was perplexed by that. Since I had no explanation for it, I got myself to a standing position and started slowly walking home.

It was the middle of summer, yet I was freezing. My entire body shook as I wrapped my arms around the front of myself, in a desperate attempt to stay warm. It wasn't working.

Over the next two weeks, I dared not leave the house. I barely even looked out the windows. I was terrified that the man would show back up again, only to succeed in carrying out his threat the next time. I dared not take any chances with Viv's life. No matter what happened to me, and no matter what I was going through, I had no right to put her life in danger. Though I truly felt that Ivy, Jack, and Harper were my true family, I still had a soft spot for Viv. No matter what, I would always think of her as my little sister.

I didn't mention my kidnapping to anyone. I didn't mention my adoption to anyone. I didn't even call Trent for an update. I jumped every time someone knocked on the front door. I was a mess.

I didn't even call Ivy. But after a while, I started to realize that she was probably worried sick about me. I told her I would get back to her right away and I never did. I'm sure she was wondering if I was all right. I wondered if she had contacted the authorities about my kidnapping yet. She knew for a fact I was alive, but didn't know where I lived who I lived with. So I really needed to call her. I waited until the family went out to run some errands and I was left alone at the house.

Before I called Ivy, there was something I was beginning to realize. My memories of her, as well as my brother and sister, were beginning to fade. It was the oddest thing. One moment, they were all I could think about. The next moment, I was having a hard time picturing Harper's face. Then it seemed as if my memories of Jack were fading. I could still see Ivy in my mind, but I was worried that would go next.

I had no idea what was happening to me, but it scared the daylights out of me. Was I going to forget them completely? It seemed to be getting worse every day. I was beginning to think that maybe I should go move in with Ivy. If I was living there, there was no way I was going to forget them. Was there?

I fought to hold on to my memories of Ivy and my siblings as tightly as I could. It was definitely a struggle. It was like a dream that you have and you remember it briefly when you first wake up. But then it fades and you completely forget about the dream. That's what I was afraid was going to happen. And it terrified me.

"Ivy?" I said when she picked up the phone.

"Oh my god, Georgie, is that you?" She sobbed into the phone. "I've been so...worried about you," she choked out between sobs.

"I know. I'm sorry. I'm okay, really. Just so much is going on over here, that I've not had a chance to call you," I lied.

I could hear her taking deep breaths on the other side of the phone. Probably in an effort to calm herself down after her outburst when she heard my voice.

CHAPTER 8

Ivy talked me into going over to her house. I was a bit hesitant at first, since I had been avoiding her for about two weeks. But it didn't matter. She welcomed me with open arms. Tears threatened to spill over. We sat down and she offered me some tea. We had a nice long talk about everything that had been going on.

In a dark restaurant across town, two men sat at a table in a far corner. Their voices were low and their eyes constantly scanning the room for eavesdroppers. No one paid them a bit of attention. The paranoia on their faces would have been obvious to anyone who cared.

The pudgy man leaned in with a whisper. "Your daughter is causing a lot of trouble for me, you know." He munched on bread and butter while waiting for the waitress to return.

"Yeah, I know," Stan replied, eyeing the couple at the next table. "I just don't know what to do about it. She's got it in her head that she can solve her kidnapping, and wants everyone to know about it. I'm at a loss as to what my next move should be."

"Your next move should be to tell her to stop. I mean immediately stop. Make yourself crystal clear. Otherwise she's going to get herself killed." The man was holding nothing back.

Stan sat back in his chair almost out of breath. "How can you say that about Georgie? She's my daughter and I love her. You wouldn't really hurt her, would you?" His eyes were bulging, with an almost inability to blink. What the man had just said to Stan absolutely terrified him.

"No, no. Of course not," the man said to Stan, waving his hand about dismissively. I would never hurt her. But there are others..." He raised his eyebrows at Stan. It was all he needed to say.

Stan shot to his feet, knocking is chair over behind him. It clanked loudly on the hard tile floor. Stan barely noticed. "I can't sit here and listened to this." His voice was loud. Almost hysterical. He glanced around the room. Quite a few pairs of eyeballs were pointed firmly in his direction.

The pudgy man patted the air in front of him. "Stan, Stan. Sit down. You are causing a scene," he said just loud enough for Stan to hear him.

Stan obeyed, picking his chair up and placing it back at the table gently. He sat. When he looked around again, most of the restaurant customers had returned to their own conversations and meals. When Stan's gaze met the couple of hangers on, they immediately turned away, having been caught staring.

"Stan, you worry me," the pudgy man said. "Getting hysterical isn't going to help anything."

"I'm hardly hysterical," Stan replied, a gruffness to his voice. "But you are threatening my daughter. I love her and won't stand for that."

"I didn't threaten her, Stan. I just informed you of what could possibly happen."

"I'm not an idiot," Stan replied. "I know a threat when I hear one."

"So, are you going to get her to keep her mouth shut, or not," the man said, ignoring Stan's last remark.

"I'll do what I can. But she's a teenager. You know teenagers," Stan told him.

"Yeah, well, just make sure she understands that this is a life or death matter."

"Okay, okay, I get it." Stan was beginning to get irritated at the man repeating over and over how his precious Georgie was in grave danger. He knew she was. He knew the man well enough to know that.

"In fact, neither of your daughters are safe at this point. You got that, right?"

Stan's eyes narrowed. His voice was slow and deliberate. "Don't you dare start threatening Viv too. She has nothing to do with this. Keep her out of it."

The pudgy man's face spread into a wide grin. "Stan, my man. I'll tell you again, I'm not threatening anyone. I'm just letting you know where everything stands. I'm not going down for any of this, without you. So, you need to make sure everyone calms down. Got it?"

Stan nodded. "Yeah, got it."

"How could you not tell me where you were all this time?" Ivy admonished. "I've been just sick about it since you left. Please don't do that to me again." The sorrow on her face shown through.

"I'm so sorry," I told her and I meant it. "I knew what I was putting her through. I just didn't know what to do about it."

"I called the sheriff, you know," Ivy told me.

My head spun around to face her. "You what? What did he say?" I was sure that the look on my face was pure terror.

"I don't know, because I hung up," she admitted. I promised you that I wouldn't call, so I couldn't go through with it. Somehow I knew that you would return."

I took in a deep breath and let it out in shudders. The thought of the sheriff's office getting involved absolutely terrified me. I knew that I was already in some danger. Obviously. I had been threatened in this lifetime and actually killed in my previous lifetime. So the idea of talking to the sheriff, and having the bad guys find out, was something I could barely handle.

What if they went after my family? Either family actually. How could I live with that? I just wanted the sheriff to stay out of it for the time being. I just felt that we were all safer that way.

"Yes, I will always return. And thank you for hanging up." I hugged my mother. "At some point I'm sure we will have to get the sheriff involved. But not just yet. Okay?"

She pulled from my hug and nodded at me. "For now, that's fine. But we can't keep this all a secret forever."

"I know," I told her. "Soon we will call him. I promise." The truth is that I wasn't absolutely sure I was going to be able to hold up that promise. But I would try. I would do anything for Ivy. I looked around. "Are Jack and Harper home?"

Ivy had no way of knowing that I desperately needed to see my brother and sister. I needed to see their faces. They seemed to be fading from my memory and it was important to me to keep them burned into my mind.

"No, sorry. They are both out," Ivy told me. "They'll be so disappointed that they missed you."

I spent the next little while telling Ivy all about my meeting with Trent.

"There's something that you should know," I told her. "It's something that I just found out from Trent."

Ivy tilted her head at me without speaking.

"Viv is also adopted."

"Really?"

Ivy did not sound surprised. But I'm sure she was. There was no way she could possibly have known that Viv was adopted. She didn't even know where I was until a couple of weeks ago. I'm sure I was imagining things.

"Yes," I confirmed. "But I don't know anything about her adoption at all. Trent didn't know anything, other than the fact that she was adopted."

"Does Viv know?" Ivy asked me.

"No. At least I'm pretty sure she doesn't know. I think she would have told me if she knew. Viv is not the type to hold things in. I'm sure of it." I explained.

"You're probably right. It makes sense that if she knew, then she would have told you," Ivy agreed.

I just remembered a promise that I made. "Do you mind if I call my...um, Beverly really quickly? I told her I would check in."

Ivy's eyebrows raised. "Does she know that you are with me?"

I shrugged. "Not exactly."

"Not exactly?" Ivy pushed a few threads of hair back that had escaped her ponytail.

"Okay, no. She doesn't know where I am." I don't know why I sounded so defensive. I'm sure she didn't mean anything by it. She just wanted to know what was going on in my life.

"So, yes, perhaps you should call her. Since we don't have any proof at this point that she was involved in your kidnapping, right now, she is just a worried mom. I've been there and don't want to be part of doing that to someone else," Ivy explained. "However, if we ever find out she was involved..." she hesitated for just a moment, "then all bets are off."

I nodded, and I agreed with her. I also didn't think that Beverly was involved in anyway whatsoever. I had no proof that she was innocent of anything, other than just my intuition.

"Hi Mom," I said into the phone to Beverly. I glanced over at Ivy, feeling a bit guilty for calling Beverly 'Mom' in front of Ivy.

Ivy just smiled back at me. I know that she got it. She understood. I was in a tight spot between two mothers. I loved them both. I had memories of them both, though very few memories of Ivy herself. Regardless, she was my mother and nothing was going to change that.

"Georgieeeeee!" Beverly screeched into the phone. "Viv is goooone!" Her words were drawn out and desperate sounding.

"What do you mean Viv is gone?" I glanced over at Ivy again, whose eyes were huge at what she had just heard me say.

"Someone took her, Georgie!" She wailed out the words.

"Okay, okay, Mom, you need to calm down and tell me exactly what happened."

I could hear her sobbing through the phone. "Yeah...all right...I...uh." She couldn't get the words out.

"Mom, take a deep breath," I encouraged.

"Viv and I were sitting here watching TV, when all of a sudden, two guys ran in through the back slider and grabbed her. I tried to hang onto her, but I couldn't." She began gasping for breath.

"Oh my god, Mom. Did you call the police?"

"I...no. You called...first." Her voice sounded confused.

I had no idea why in the world she hadn't called the police first. It seemed to me like she would call Stan and the police immediately.

"Mom, you need to call the police."

"I thought maybe you knew something. That's why I'm talking to you first," she told me.

"Me? What would I know?"

"I don't know exactly. But, you have been saying that you were kidnapped, and asking a lot of questions. I just thought it might be related," Beverly tried to explain.

It wasn't a bad theory. It was entirely possible that this was related to me. In fact, it was quite likely. The fact that I was going around asking questions, and bothering people, and even being chased down and threatened, told me that this probably was my fault.

"You might be right, Mom. I'm coming home. Call the police and Dad right now. And in that order. I'll be there as soon as I can." I hung up the phone and turned to Ivy. "Can you give me a ride home? It will take too long to get there by bus."

I knew that by asking Ivy to give me a ride home, I was exposing where I lived and who I lived with. But we were past all of that. I had to take my chances that she wouldn't call the police and get them involved just yet. However, with what just happened to Viv, it might be too late to worry about any of that.

"Of course." Ivy grabbed her purse. "Let's go."

Ivy began racing through the streets of town, heading out of Red Lake. I hung on tightly as she spun around the corners in an effort to get me home as quickly as possible.

"Ivy, please. Slow down. If you kill us, we won't get there at all."

She looked over at me. "Sorry. I was just trying to help."

Ivy looked over and could see how upset I was. It was very important to me to get home and help figure out what happened to Viv.

As she was looking at me, neither one of us noticed that she rolled right through a red light. Until it was too late.

The huge black SUV slammed into us right at the driver's side door, causing us to go into an uncontrollable slide. When we hit the edge of the roadway, our car rolled over several times. I don't think either one of us had taken the time to put on a seatbelt. We had been in such a hurry. We were being thrown around the car, and every time I hit something, I felt a bone break.

That's the last thing I remember.

PART 3

CHAPTER 1

"Mommy, wake up!" I could feel someone tugging at my arm. I pulled it away. All I wanted to do was sleep. "Mommy!"

Very carefully, I partially opened my eyes to see who it was that was bothering me. A small child stood in front of me. He couldn't have been more than four or five years old. He was a cute little guy with strawberry blond hair and bright green eyes. He smiled when I looked at him. I couldn't help but smile back.

Whose kid was this, I wondered?

"Mommy, get up," he said again. "I'm hungry."

"Kid, you have the wrong person. I'm not your...Oh my god!"

My eyes flew open and I sat straight up in the bed. The oxygen escaped my lungs. My head bolted around looking at everything in the room, trying to recognize something to make sense of it all. But none of it made sense. I had no idea where I was. I had no idea who the child standing in front of me was.

The room was painted a pretty yellowish color, with white trim. The lace curtains were sheer and didn't block much of the light coming into the room. Because of that, the room was very bright. I had no idea how I had managed to sleep. I was a light sleeper and normally the brightness would have awakened me at the crack of dawn.

My mind went immediately to Ivy and the car we were driving in. We had been in an accident. Obviously, I was all right, but what about Ivy? Did she make it? Why didn't I remember anything else?

Did someone carry me here from the car accident to recuperate? Why didn't they call an ambulance? I was very confused.

Oh, and Viv. Where was she? I needed to get up and go home and find out what was going on with Viv.

"Hun, are you going to get up and get Taylor some breakfast?" The voice was coming from another room.

Was he talking to me? He couldn't be. Though the voice did sound familiar, I couldn't place it. I needed to get up and get dressed and get out of there. I found some clothes that I didn't recognize, but they looked about my size, hanging over a chair across the room. I told the little boy to leave the room while I quickly got dressed. He obliged, with a pout.

"Georgie, did you hear me?" The voice was more insistent that time. He was talking to me. Still, I couldn't place the voice.

I walked out into the living room. There sat Tommy Vaughn, my childhood friend. But he looked a lot older.

"What are you doing here?" I asked him. "Why am I here? What is going on?"

He scrunched up his face a bit. "What do you mean?"

"Why do you look so much older…" I gasped, as it felt like a lightning bolt hit me. Oh no.

Was it happening again? I ran to the bathroom to look in the mirror. I could hear Tommy calling after me.

"Georgie, are you okay?"

"Um, yeah, I'm fine," I called back, slamming the door behind me.

My face was older. Not a lot. But probably eight or ten years. I was definitely in my twenties. Not the 15 year old that had just been in a horrific car accident with Ivy. It had happened again. I had died. I knew that. And here I was, several years older. I always seemed to wake up confused, causing me to not realize what was going on for a few minutes. This time was no different.

Now what? And why was Tommy here? And that little boy?

"What are you doing here?" I asked Tommy when I finally worked up the nerve to leave the safety of the bathroom.

"Why wouldn't I be here? I live here," he told me matter of factly. "What is going on with you?"

"Mommy." I felt a tug on my t-shirt.

We both turned to the child. "And why does that little boy keep calling me that?" I braced for his answer.

"Because you are his mother," Tommy replied. He climbed off of the sofa and walked over to me, putting the back of his hand on my forehead. I moved back a pace, out of reach. He dropped his arm to his side, with a scowl. "Do you have a fever?" he asked me.

"No, I don't have a fever. That kid is not mine. I'm only 15 years..." Oh wait. Crap. Maybe he is. How can I not remember such a life altering event. "So does that mean you and I are...?" I couldn't bring myself to say it.

"Married? Yeah, we're married. We have been for seven years now. What is going on with you Georgie?"

I shook my head "You wouldn't believe me if I told you. I do have a question for you. Several actually."

"Um, okay," he replied.

"Is Ivy okay?"

"Who?" he asked.

"Mommy, I'm hungry." It was the little boy...my son, again. Wow that was weird to say. I have a son.

Tommy turned to him. "Come on Taylor, I'll get you some cereal. Mommy isn't feeling well right now." Tommy looked up and scowled at me as he ushered our son toward the kitchen.

"Taylor," I repeated. "Why did we name him that?"

"It's your maiden name. We thought it would be a great name for him. Georgie, you need to tell me what's going on with you."

"Oh." Well, that answers some questions. Clearly, I was adopted in this lifetime by Stan and Beverly Taylor again. So where were they? And where was Ivy? Oh, and where was Viv? Had she been kidnapped? If so, was she back? I had a million questions that I needed answers for.

I paced the living room while I waited for Tommy to return. I felt like a caged animal. We needed to talk. After what seemed like an eternity, he came back in with a concerned look on his face.

"Georgie, what's…"

I grabbed his hand and pulled him to the couch, not giving him a chance to finish asking his question. I knew what he was going to say. There was no point in him asking any questions. I needed to be the one asking questions.

Tommy sat down next to me with big eyes. I was acting weird. I knew it. He knew it. But I didn't care.

"Is Viv all right? I mean, is she alive?"

Tommy scrunched up his eyebrows. "Georgie, why would you ask me that?"

"Tommy, please." I took his hands in mine and held them tight. "Can you please just answer me? This is important."

He looked down at his hands, and pulled them out of my death grip. "Damn, Georgie, what's gotten into you?" He shook his hands in the air in a dramatic attempt to get the circulation back in them.

"Tommy!"

He looked me directly in the eyes. "Yeah, okay, sorry. Yes, Viv is fine. Now are you going to tell me what this is all about?"

I let out a deep breath of relief.

Now I needed to know if Ivy was okay. But when I asked

him a few minutes prior, he seemed to have no idea who she was. That told me volumes. Ivy was not in my life this time. Why? Was I aware of being kidnapped and adopted prior to waking up in this lifetime? It didn't seem like it. Tommy seemed like he had no idea what I was talking about.

"I'll explain later. I promise. Okay?" I told him. I threw some sad eyes his way, hoping that would appease him for a little while at least.

"Yeah, okay. I'm going to take Taylor to the park," he replied. "Do you want to come?"

"No," I said a little too fast. "I mean, next time for sure. I just don't feel very well right now. I think I'll lie down for a while." I looked over at the couch as I spoke.

I noticed just the slightest of eye rolls from my husband. "Yeah, fine. Come on Taylor, get your shoes on."

Once they left, I made myself a bowl of cereal and perched myself on a barstool to contemplate what to do next.

This living my lives over thing was beginning to wear thin. I had no idea what was causing it and no earthly idea what to do to stop it. I didn't want to die permanently. I just wanted to live out a normal life. I knew it was a family trait, based on what Ivy had told me previously. Even though it had happened to her many times, she still didn't know what to do about it either.

Ivy did tell me that every time she came back, she needed to save her friends from dying, and she needed to stop the serial killer who was killing them. Once she accomplished everything, which took several lifetimes, she never died and came back again. She is living her final life, as far as she knows.

That got me to wondering. If I was able to solve my own kidnapping, and Viv's kidnapping also, as well as figure out who was trying to kill me, this whole horrific ordeal might stop. It might be over forever. I could only hope.

One thing I was pretty sure about, was that whoever was involved in my kidnapping, was almost certainly the same person who was trying to kill me. Or at least part of the same group of people.

Now, how to figure that out...

After finishing my breakfast, I found a telephone hanging on the wall. I smiled at that. It was pretty rare to find a wall-mounted telephone anymore. But I didn't see a cell phone lying around. So the wall phone would have to do. I had committed Ivy's phone number to memory.

"Hello?"

Aw dang, I hadn't even thought about what I would actually say. I quickly realized that Ivy and I had not had a conversation in this lifetime. She would be shocked and maybe a bit freaked out by receiving a phone call from me.

"Hello, is anyone there?"

"Um, hi." It was all I could manage to spit out.

"Hi," Ivy replied. "Can I help you?"

Her voice was so kind. It was what I remembered best about her. Even so, I panicked and hung up. I just had not thought the phone call through. I didn't know how to broach the subject.

So there I sat. I needed to come up with a better plan than calling my mother and hanging up on her. I also considered going to see Viv. But what would I say? She would be a grown woman now, not the young teen that I remembered.

But Viv would have to wait. I knew what I needed to do.

CHAPTER 2

An hour later, I found myself standing on Ivy's doorstep. There was no time to waste. I might not be alive the next day. I needed to take care of things now. Right now.

I had found what I assumed was my car, in the garage of my house. Even after my drive to Red Lake, I was completely unaware of what I was going to say to her. But Ivy was the only one that I really felt I could trust at this point. So far, I had no contact with Stanley, Beverly, or Viv, and I didn't know how they would react to any of this. My kidnapping, my adoption, any of it. So I wanted to start with Ivy.

"Hi." There I go again, with nothing more interesting to say, but 'hi.'

"Hi, can I help...oh my god." Ivy's face went pale and I noticed her holding on tightly to the door knob. It looked as if she was about to faint.

"Are you okay?" I asked, stepping up to the door and putting my hand on her arm, to steady her. She was clammy and shaking. I patted her arm in an attempt to calm her down a bit. I noticed even her breathing was labored.

"Yeah...I...are you...?" She couldn't get the words out. But I knew exactly what she was going to say. She recognized me.

"Yes. I'm Georgie."

She looked around frantically. "I need to sit."

Just like the last time I showed up on her doorstep, I guided her over to the bench seat on her front porch. She sat down gently and bent over, almost touching her forehead to her knees. I just sat next to her, and let her take it all in.

This time she did not sob. It was more of a quiet acknowledgment of my existence. She just needed to gather herself before speaking with me.

"I can't believe this is happening." She finally sat up straight and looked me in the eyes.

I nodded. "I know. But it's really me."

"Yes, I know it's you. I knew that the second I saw you," she admitted. "It's just been so long, you know?"

"I know."

"Where have you been all these years? I had no idea if you were dead or alive." It was a legitimate question.

"I've been living with a nice family, not too far from here." It was the truth.

"How did you end up with them? I thought maybe you had been mur..." She couldn't bring herself to say it.

"No, clearly I wasn't murdered. I was adopted."

"Adopted? Why would someone kidnap you and then just give you to someone to adopt? You know you were kidnapped, right?" she asked.

"I know. And I'll tell you the whole sordid story. What I know of it anyway. But first, I want to let you know, that we just talked recently. In my previous lifetime, that is." I bit my lower lip, expecting a...

Ivy gasped. Yep, there it was.

"Your previous life? So you live your lives over and over, like me?"

"Yes, just like you. You once told me that it was the family curse," I explained.

Ivy smiled. "Yes, that is what I call it. I'm so happy that we have seen each other recently, even if I don't remember it."

"Yeah me too."

That's when I went on to tell her all about my life experiences, and my deaths. I told her about my adopted family, Stan, Beverly, and mostly about Viv. There was just something about that girl that made her the awesome person that she was.

Ivy reached up and brushed her hand along the length of my red hair. "You've turned into such a beautiful young woman."

"There's something I haven't told you about this lifetime," I added to my story. "I have a husband and a son."

Her eyebrows shot up. "I have a grandchild? Oh that's so fantastic. This has become a day of miracles."

"I don't know them though," I explained. "I mean, I know Tommy, my husband. We grew up together. His family are friends of my parents." I gave her an apologetic look for calling someone else my parents.

She knew. "It's okay. As far as you are concerned, they are your parents. Unless they are the ones who kidnapped you. Are they?"

I shook my head. "I don't think so. I think they were part of the fraud and kidnapping, without knowing it."

"I see." Ivy looked over my shoulder, off in the distance. She seemed to have something deep on her mind. Of course she would. Who wouldn't in her position?

"Are you all right?" I asked, snapping Ivy out of her daydream.

She met my eyes. "Yes, of course. I'm just thrilled that you are here."

"You know, as much as it pains me to say this, I think that I should go back to my husband and son, and try to figure out what happened. Find out who my kidnapper is, all of it."

"Really?" She was shocked that I wanted to leave her. Especially since she hadn't seen me in well over 20 years.

"Yes," I told her. "We could call the sheriff and start an investigation. Or maybe even the FBI, since it was a kidnapping case. But, it's been so long. The thing is that I'm closest to all of them. I'm an adult now, thank goodness. I was only 15 last time. But this time I can do some research, ask some questions, without being accused of acting like an hysterical teenager."

"Oh, Georgie, I don't know. It sounds dangerous, and I don't think I would survive losing you again."

I took her hands in mine. "I'll be fine. Really."

I didn't know if that was the case at all. It seemed as if dying was what I did best. Ivy reluctantly let me go. Once again, I hadn't told her exactly who I was living with and where I lived. I didn't want her to go to the police and ruin everything. This was something I needed to do on my own.

I headed back to the home that I shared with Tommy and Taylor. It was very strange that I had a husband and a child. At least I remembered Tommy from my previous life.

CHAPTER 3

Tommy accosted me the moment I arrived home. "Where have you been? We've been worried sick!" He shook his head at me as he spoke.

I was taken aback by the abruptness of it all. I wasn't used to having anyone jump on me like that. Especially a husband. He really needed to tread lightly. This husband thing was all very new to me.

I couldn't help but get a bit defensive. "I'm sorry, but do I have to answer to you?" It came out snarkier than I had planned.

He gave me the side eye. "No, of course you don't have to answer to me. We were just worried, that's all. You usually are courteous enough to at least let me know where you are going. Just so I don't worry."

My hand flew up in the air between us. "Okay, okay, I get it. You were worried. I'll try to keep you informed of my comings and goings from now on."

Ugh, I hated that idea. I have never had a husband before. This whole thing was completely new to me. I wasn't used to getting permission to do things. Well... I guess I had to get permission from my parents to do things. But that was different. They were my parents. A life partner was supposed to be somebody I wanted to be with. Not somebody I had to answer to. I would have to work on figuring it all out.

Tommy's face fell. I had hurt him. I could see that. I needed to fix things. I couldn't be in this lifetime with a husband that I didn't get along with. Besides, I remembered Tommy being a really nice guy. Though, admittedly, I didn't know what kind of a husband he was.

"Please, let's sit," I asked of him, turning to the couch. "Where's the little boy?"

"You mean our son?" I could hear the annoyance in his voice.

Oops. "Yeah, sorry. Where's Taylor?" I asked.

"He's next door, playing. Bridgett's mother will bring him back in a little while."

"Oh, okay," I responded, having no idea who Bridgett or her mother were. "I need to talk to you in private anyway."

"What about? Your crazy behavior today?" he asked.

"Well...yes," I answered honestly.

Tommy sat down in the soft leather chair across from me on the couch. "Okay, here I am. So, what gives?"

"Okay, well...I need to tell you something about myself," I began.

"Yeah?"

"I don't remember you...wait. I do remember you. What I mean is that I don't remember marrying you. I only remember you as a teenager, when we were friends," I tried to explain.

"What do you mean?" He didn't sound like he believed me. Well, who would?

"I keep dying and reliving my life. This is my fifth life. I think." I looked at the wall behind my husband, counting my lives in my head. Once that was done, I met his gaze. "Yeah, five. And I have no idea how many more times this is going to happen."

Tommy had a blank look on his face, with no indication of

whether he believed a word I was saying or not. My best guess is that he didn't believe a word of it. And that would not surprise me whatsoever.

I decided to continue. "And I don't remember Taylor. In fact, I just woke up this morning, in our bed, after having died yesterday."

Tommy jumped up out of his chair, walking around behind it. "Is this a joke? Because I don't find it very funny."

I shook my head. "No, it is absolutely not a joke. Heaven knows that I wish it was. This whole thing is a nightmare actually. Believe me when I tell you that I just want a normal life. Not this crazy thing that is happening to me, over and over again."

"Georgie, how can you possibly expect me to believe any of your story?" he replied. "Do you know how crazy you sound?"

"Of course I know how crazy it sounds. I've run all of this through my head more times than I would like to count. Yes, it's completely crazy," I answered honestly.

"I just don't know what you expect me to do with this story of yours."

He didn't believe any of it. Not that I really expected him to. Hell, I barely believed it, and it was happening to me. Ignoring his last comment, I continued.

"Can we talk about my adoption?" I asked him, kind of changing the subject.

"Yeah, what about it?" he asked. He was beginning to sound a bit hostile. I had no choice but to let it slide.

"I'm pretty sure that I was kidnapped at three years old. No...I'm positive of it," I told him.

"What do you mean? You weren't kidnapped. You were adopted. I don't understand what you are trying to tell me," Tommy answered.

"When I was three years old, I lived with my biological family. My mother's name is Ivy Wells. I also have an older brother and sister. Jack and Harper. We were at a picnic at the lake, when someone took me. Then the Taylor family adopted me." I sat back on the couch, fearing the response I was inevitably going to receive.

"That never happened, Georgie. Your parents would never be involved in a kidnapping." He scoffed at me.

"I didn't say they were involved. In fact, I'm sure they weren't. At least as far as I know, they weren't involved." It made me wonder though. Could they have been involved? I guess that it was possible.

"So...if your parents weren't involved in kidnapping you, how do you suppose you ended up with them? I mean, if someone kidnaps a child, don't they do it so they can keep the kid?" he asked.

"Ivy thinks there was a black market baby ring involved."

"Wait...you've talked to that woman? Are you out of your mind? She might be crazy," he admonished. "In fact, she probably is, if she's telling you stories like that. You know she's not really your mother, right?"

"Hey!" I defended. "She's not crazy! She is my mother." I couldn't help but get angry at his accusations.

"You don't know that!" he yelled back.

I flew off of the couch. "Yes I do!"

We both turned at the sound of a knock on the front door. Tommy glared at me as he walked over and opened the door.

"Mommy!" Taylor ran inside and grabbed me around the waist. I reciprocated with a hug back. He was a young boy. He would never understand any of this mess that I had found myself part of.

Tommy said a few words to Bridgett's mother, who waved at me as she turned and left.

"We will finish this conversation later," Tommy said to me with a sweet voice, for Taylor's benefit.

"I'm going to go lie down," I told him. "This whole thing is giving me a headache."

Tommy didn't respond as he walked Taylor into the kitchen for an afternoon snack. I walked to our bedroom and closed the door behind me. I even locked it. I didn't care if Tommy thought that was weird, or if it made him angry. I just wanted some privacy.

Pulling back the covers, I crawled into the inviting warmth of the bed. It was the only place I felt comfortable at the moment. In the morning, I would go see Viv. I missed her and wanted to make sure she was all right.

CHAPTER 4

A little while later, I woke up, feeling refreshed. Opening the bedroom door, I was surprised to find it unlocked, knowing for a fact I had left it locked. But I didn't think much beyond that. Maybe Tommy had come in while I was sleeping to check on me and left it unlocked.

I looked around the house. Tommy and Taylor were nowhere to be found. Perhaps Tommy had just taken our son out for dinner, since I was still asleep. I went to the refrigerator and made myself a sandwich to tide me over until they arrived back home.

I thought about calling Ivy, but decided to wait. I wanted to do a little bit of investigating and see what I could find out. I wanted to give her some actual good news for a change. I looked through our book collection on the shelf in the living room. Lots of horror. Those had to be Tommy's books. Horror was really not my thing. I liked mysteries and dramas. I pulled out a book called 'Winters Legend on Stone Mountain.' After reading the summary on the back cover, it sounded perfect. I nestled into the corner of the couch and began reading.

But my mind was wandering. The book was interesting, but

I just could not concentrate. I sat there on the couch for at least another 20 minutes, lost in thought. I needed to figure out what to do. Tommy didn't believe anything I said, so he was out when it came to people helping me. Viv didn't know anything about what was going on. In fact I hadn't even seen her in this lifetime. Ivy was the only one I could really talk to. She understood me. She understood everything I was going through. Just as I stood up to give Ivy a call, the front door opened. It was early evening and the room was a bit shadowy.

"Oh, you're up," Tommy said to me.

"Yeah, I haven't been up long, I..." I stopped mid sentence when someone else walked in behind Tommy. "Who is this?"

Before Tommy had a chance to answer me, I could feel all the blood rushing from my face.

"Georgie, are you all right?" Tommy rushed over and took my arm, guiding me to sit back down on the couch. "You look like you are about to faint."

"Mom?"

Oh god, that confirmed it. The teenage boy standing in front of me was Taylor. He was no longer a cute little four year old. He looked like he was 14 or 15 at this point. The gold ring in his lip glistened in the lamp light. I caught myself staring and had to force my eyes back up into his.

I looked at Tommy for answers. What the hell had just happened? I didn't die. At least I don't think I did. All I did was lie down to take a nap. Then I woke up, what, ten years later?

I turned to Taylor. "How old are you?"

He scrunched up his face and tilted his head at me. "Mom, you know how old I am. What is wrong with you?"

"Please just answer the question."

"I'm 14, Mom. You know that."

I nodded. Yeah, it had been about ten years since I had laid down for that nap. Now what I needed to know was if I was in the same lifetime that I laid down to take that nap in? Or was this an entirely new lifetime? And how in the world was I going to figure the answer out to that one?

Oh, it dawned on me. Ivy. If I contact her and she remembers talking to me ten years ago, then I will know that I'm in the same lifetime. If I contact her and she hasn't seen me since I was three years old, then I must have died and restarted.

"I'll get you some water, Mom." Taylor disappeared toward the kitchen.

Tommy sat down on the couch next to me. "Are you okay? You look like you've seen a ghost."

Once Tommy was seated so close to me, I could see his face much more clearly. He was no longer that fresh faced mid 20s guy that I remembered. Now he must be in his mid-30s. Laugh lines were starting to form around his eyes and mouth. He was aging well, but I could definitely see it.

"Here you go, Mom."

Taylor handed me the water and I drank it slowly. I was biding my time, while I thought about what I was going to do about all of it. I came up with nothing during the full minute I dragged out that drink.

"Mom, are you all right?"

"Yes, guys, I'm fine. I guess I was just startled at the two of you walking in like that. Sorry."

"Why did you ask who I was? And how old I am?" There were tears threatening to spill down Taylor's face.

I patted my son's hand. "I'm sorry, honey. I guess I'm just out of it from my nap. You don't need to worry about me now. Really. I'm fine. Um, Taylor, why don't you go on to your room? Your dad and I need to talk. Okay?"

"Yeah, okay. Let me know if you need me though." Taylor turned and headed down the hallway, turning back once or twice to look at me. He was worried. Who can blame a son for that?

Tommy stroked my arm, lovingly. "Georgie, what is going on? Are you sick?"

I shook my head. "No, I'm not sick. I need to talk to you though."

I had to try telling Tommy once again what was going on with me. Last time he didn't believe a word I said, but maybe this time would be different. I didn't know what else to do. I felt like it was necessary.

"Okay, here goes. I don't know if you are going to believe me or not, but please try to keep an open mind."

"Yeah, okay."

"I keep dying and coming back. I'm reliving my life over and over." I bit my bottom lip, fearing his reaction.

"Seriously? Not this again."

"Wait, what? I've told you this before?"

"Yeah, back when Taylor was really young. Maybe four or five years old. I don't remember exactly when. You don't remember telling me?"

Holy crap. That meant that I did not die. If I had, he would not remember us having that conversation. To me, that conversation was only a few hours ago, before I laid down for a nap. To him, it was ten years ago. If I didn't die, then how in the world did I take a nap and wake up ten years later? That was a completely new one. And I had no idea how to handle it. If I told Ivy about it, I think that would be a new one on her too. Because she never once mentioned anything like that to me.

"Well, yeah, I do remember telling you. But, now please bear with me, right after that conversation, I took a nap, and woke up just now, ten years later. I don't remember a thing in between."

Tommy paused, I'm sure that he was contemplating the crazy story I had just told him. "How can that be? You have been awake and alert all of this time. You don't remember anything from those years at all?"

"Not a thing."

"I need to take you to the hospital." He stood and reached for my hand. "Come on, let's go."

I pulled my hand back from his. "No. I don't need the hospital. I'm not sick. I'm not crazy. At least, I don't think I am." I realized how insane that actually sounded.

Tommy sat back down next to me. "You know what? I'm just tired of all this drama. You tell me that you are reliving your lives. You tell me that you were kidnapped as a child and adopted out, by god knows who. Now you tell me that you just don't remember anything from the past ten years. How am I supposed to react to all of this?"

He looked at me like I had the answers. I didn't. I didn't know the answer to any of those questions. And once again, Tommy didn't believe a word I was saying. What was I even doing in this marriage? I clearly had a husband that didn't trust me and thought I was losing my mind. Hell, maybe I was. But I honestly didn't think that was the case.

Regardless of the fact that I was falling asleep and waking up in unfamiliar territory, I was losing time. I have gained 20 years in a matter of days. At this rate I would be an old woman in a week. That horrified me. That was a way worse fate than dying and coming back again. At least I was still young each time that happened. But once I became an old woman, I wondered if it was even possible to come back younger.

I decided to let everything just kind of calm down, for the time being at least. I told Tommy that I was letting it go. I didn't promise him it would be forever. I told him that for right now I would leave it alone. I figured I would give it a week. I wouldn't do anything at all during that time. At that point, I would have to see what was going on. I just wanted to keep the peace with my husband. I might have to live with him for a very long time.

CHAPTER 5

One week passed by in a blur and I kept my promise. I did not contact Ivy at all. I honestly thought it might kill me though. I couldn't concentrate. I couldn't do anything that didn't involve thinking about talking with Ivy.

Since it had been a week, I figured that I had waited long enough. I would call Ivy in the morning. Of course, I didn't get a wink of sleep that night. Tommy laid next to me, snoring like a chainsaw. I just stared at the ceiling. The moment that I noticed the horizon just beginning to lighten, I sprung out of bed. Not that I would even consider calling Ivy that early, but at least I was up out of bed and away from just staring at the ceiling.

Finally, Tommy left for work, and Taylor headed for a friend's house. The moment I saw Tommy's car pull out of the driveway, I rushed to the phone and dialed the phone number that I had committed to memory in a previous lifetime. I prayed that Ivy still had the same number after all the years, and lifetimes, that had passed.

I recognized Harper's voice the moment that she answered. Oh boy, I hadn't thought about what I would say to anyone else that answered. I just assumed Ivy would. Harper would be about

42 years old now. I'm sure she had long ago accepted the fact that I was never going to come home. What was I going to say to her? Who was I going to say that I was?

"Hello, is anyone there?" Harper said when I didn't immediately respond.

"Oh yeah, sorry. Is Ivy home?"

"No. Who is this?" Why did her voice sound so accusatory?

"Just a friend." I guess it wasn't totally a lie.

"If you are a friend, then you know she isn't home," Harper spouted. "Are you a bill collector?"

"What? No. Can you just tell me when she will be back?"

"She's not coming back. She's dead."

With that, she slammed the phone down and there was nothing but silence. I pulled it away from my ear and looked at the receiver in astonishment. What Harper just told me can't be true. Maybe she was just angry about me calling for some reason. And maybe she just didn't want me calling back, because she thought I was a bill collector.

I hung up the phone gently. Now what? I needed to find out if Ivy really was dead, or if Harper was lying to me. I walked over to the computer and did a search for the death of Ivy Wells.

Oh my god, there it was. An obituary. Ivy's obituary. Before I even had a chance to read it, I started breathing heavily and everything around me started going dark. I landed with a thud on the living room floor.

I woke with a gasp, my head pounding, still lying on the living room floor. My first thought was whether I was still in the same lifetime or not. Apparently falling asleep, or maybe even passing out, was enough to make me either start a new lifetime or wake up several years older.

I pulled myself up into a sitting position, and rubbed my temples. I don't think my head has ever hurt so badly in my entire life. After a few minutes of that, I managed to stand up and make my way to the bathroom. Looking in the mirror, I looked the same. So I was pretty sure that I had not aged while I was passed out.

I wandered into our bedroom and found the same pajamas lying on the bed that I had changed out of that morning. The yellow flannel, with white polka dots. Okay, I was convinced that it was the same day. Thankfully.

Then it hit me. Ivy was dead. I sat down in front of the computer, to take it all in. I hadn't had a chance to do that before, I passed out so quickly from the shock, I guess.

Someone had shot Ivy as she was leaving her home just a few days prior. What the hell? Who would do that? She never hurt anyone. The killer was still at large.

I wondered if it was my fault. Was I asking too many questions? Was I riling up the wrong people? I was horrified to think that I could be responsible for Ivy's death. But what else could it be? I couldn't think of a single other reason for someone to kill Ivy, if it didn't have to do with my kidnapping. The strange thing was that I hadn't even talked to Ivy in this lifetime. So that made it unlikely that I was the cause. But I had to be. Somehow... I had to be responsible.

Now what?

Before I had a chance to even think about what to do next, the telephone rang.

"Hello?"

"I know everything. I know who killed Ivy Wells. I know who kidnapped you and your sister." I didn't recognize the voice on the other end of the line. "Meet me at the park in 30 minutes."

"You know who killed my mother? Who is this?"

Before I heard the answer, something hard struck me in the back of the head and I went down.

CHAPTER 6

"Georgie, are you all right? Wake up." It was Tommy's voice.

"Mmm, yeah. I think so."

My head was pounding from the blow I had just received. I struggled to stay conscious. I reached around to the back of my head to see how large the lump was.

"Georgie, get up. I'm worried about you." Tommy reached for my hand before I could feel for the lump. He pulled me up into a sitting position.

I looked around me. I was in our room, in bed. How did I get there? Maybe Tommy found me on the floor and carried me in. I could see it was late afternoon, by the shadows pushing their way in through the slats of the bedroom window shades.

"Um, is Taylor here? I want to make sure he's okay. I think I scared him the other day."

Tommy narrowed his eyes. "What do you mean? How did you scare him?"

"You know, when I acted as if I didn't know who he was. I was just surprised to see him as a teenager, that's all."

"Georgie, Taylor is not a teenager. He's 24 years old, and married. His wife is expecting." I could hear the disgust in

Tommy's voice. "It's been ten years since your 'episode.' Please tell me this isn't happening again."

I managed to make my way to the bathroom mirror. "Oh god. No." I was in my mid forties. Middle aged. My knees gave way and I slumped to the hard tile floor.

"Georgie!" I heard Tommy running toward me.

It was all I could do to keep myself conscious. There was no way I was going to let myself pass out again. If I did, I might wake up at 80 years old next time. I just couldn't handle that. I pushed myself up to a seated position, and Tommy sat down on the floor next to me, cradling me as I cried.

"Tommy, I don't know what to do. I keep losing decades of my life. Each time I wake up I'm something like ten years older. How old am I now?"

"You're 45. And you are about to become a grandmother. I don't understand how you can't remember all these past years."

"I know, Tommy. I don't understand it either. I need to do something to stop this. If I don't, I'm going to die of old age before I know it. The problem is that I don't have the first clue as to what to do. It just keeps happening and I can't stop it."

That's when all of the emotion spilled out of me. The two of us sat there on that bathroom floor for probably an hour, while I cried and blubbered into his arms. I have to admit, that he was very understanding about the whole thing. He hadn't been in the past, but this time seemed to be different.

When I finally calmed down and my breathing was no longer in shuddering gasps, we got up and walked into the living room.

I turned to Tommy. "The last time, you know like ten years ago, I was hit on the head by a heavy object and was knocked unconscious."

"Yeah, I remember that. I came home and found you on the floor. We went to the hospital and they said you had a concussion. You were fine though. You don't remember anything after that?"

"Not a thing. I do remember what happened right before I was hit though," I told him. "Someone called me and said that they knew who killed my mother."

"Your mother is still alive, Georgie. You just talked to Beverly yesterday."

"No, not Beverly. I'm talking about my bio mom, Ivy."

"Oh. Her." His voice was dripping with disgust. "Yeah, you did tell me about that. She was shot, if I remember correctly."

I decided to let the tone in his voice go. "Yes, that's what I read. Did they ever find out who did it?"

"No, I don't think so. At least you've never mentioned it." Tommy headed for the kitchen. "You hungry?"

"Tommy, wait. There's more. The person who called also said they knew who kidnapped me and Viv."

"Right. I remember you telling me that too." He opened the refrigerator, bending over to peruse its contents. "But you didn't know who it was and they never called back." He stood. "We don't have anything decent to eat. Want to go out for dinner?"

I let out a deep breath. "Sure, I guess. But this all sucks. Here I am, back in the same boat, something like ten...no 20, years ago. I don't know anything. And now I can't even call Ivy to help me."

Tommy walked over and wrapped his arms around me. "Honey, just let it go. It's been over 40 years since all that mess started. Your kidnapping, if that happened at all, and your adoption. I don't think you are going to find out anything at this point." He rubbed the salt and pepper stubble on his chin. "Hell, probably everyone involved is dead anyway."

I narrowed my eyes his way. I didn't like that, even after all of the time that had passed, he still didn't believe I was kidnapped. He was probably right though. But it didn't make me feel any better.

CHAPTER 7

The very next morning, Tommy took Taylor out for a father-son overnight camping trip. It was just what I needed. Having to field questions and accusations from Tommy was getting tedious.

The moment they left, I headed to my parents' house. At dinner, Tommy had filled me in on the family over the last ten years, since I had been 'gone.'

My father, Stanley, had died a couple years prior. Apparently, he was sitting at a stoplight, when someone jumped into the passenger door of his car, and stabbed him. Yeah, stabbed him.

What the hell was going on? Everybody seemed to be dying around me. Could that just be an unfortunate coincidence? Or was he targeted, because of me? Tommy did say that I continued asking question over the years, never really giving up on finding out my story. Though I don't remember any of that.

I was curious if I had actually found anything out. I did a little bit of searching in the house for notes and other paperwork. I didn't find anything.

Only my mother was at home when I arrived. I don't know

why I expected anything else. Viv was a grown woman with a family of her own and wouldn't be living at my mother's house. My mother and I sat down and had a long talk. I once again went over everything I knew with her. She remembered me telling her about being kidnapped and all that. But she didn't know anything new. She was going to be a dead end. I needed to find a new lead somewhere.

As I was walking out the door, my father-in-law, Trent, walked in. He had aged quite a bit. Of course he had. It had been decades since I remembered seeing him last. He must have been at least 70. Other than the obvious signs of aging, he was still the short, portly man I remembered. He had put on a few more pounds, and his jowls bounced as he walked. Otherwise, he was still Trent.

"Georgie, my girl, how are you?" Trent wrapped me in an all enveloping hug. I thought I might suffocate in the layers of fat.

He finally released me and I struggled not to sound like I was trying to catch my breath, while we exchanged pleasantries.

"Oh, I'm just running some errands. Tommy and Taylor went camping, so I've got a lot of free time on my hands."

"Yeah, Tommy told me," Trent replied. "He actually invited me along for a multi-generational camping trip, I guess." He laughed then. "It would probably be fun hanging out in the woods with my son and grandson. But seriously, can you imagine me camping? And hiking?" His portly belly jiggled in response to his howl of laughter at that one.

I couldn't help but laugh back along with him. It was a bit ludicrous to imagine him doing anything outdoorsy at all. And hiking? Just no.

"So, Bev...um Mom, I'll come by later in the week for lunch, okay?"

She hugged me. "Perfect, hun, talk to you later."

"Bye, Georgie." Trent waved as I closed the door behind me.

I knew that Trent had been a family friend for many

decades, but I still found it a bit odd that he was visiting my mother. I always thought of him as more of my father's friend. But perhaps, he came by and checked on my mother from time to time since Stanley's untimely death. I would have to ask Tommy about it.

I stopped just outside the front door to fish my car keys from my purse. They were lost somewhere in the abyss, along with some questionable items. I even found a pocket knife in there. That was weird, and not like me at all.

Finally locating my keys, I pulled them out and held them up in front of me in victory. I just laughed at myself as I turned to make the descent down the porch steps. But the voices inside caught my attention. It wasn't my intention to eavesdrop, but that's what happened anyway. Once I heard them speaking, I couldn't help but listen in.

"So, how is my baby girl doing these days?" Trent asked Beverly. "I haven't seen her around in ages."

His 'baby girl?' Was that a nickname for me? Or someone else? I pressed my ear to the front door. I thought Tommy was an only child. Perhaps he meant it just as a term of endearment, not his literal baby girl.

"Oh, she's doing fine. The kids are keeping her hopping."

Who were they talking about? They certainly weren't talking about me. I only had one child, Taylor. I set my purse down on the front porch, as quietly as possible, so I could concentrate on the conversation happening just feet away from me.

"Has Viv been by lately? Can you let me know when she will be over next?" Trent asked. "I miss my baby girl and would love to see her."

"Don't call her your 'baby girl.' She's my daughter now." Beverly's voice suddenly changed to mama bear. "She comes by now and then." There was a pause. "You aren't going to tell her, are you? Not after all this time."

My eyes widened. Tell her what?

"No, of course not. She just lost Stan a couple years back. She doesn't need to know that I'm her real father. I wouldn't do that to her. Or to you, for that matter."

Her what?! Trent is Viv's biological father! What the hell! I knew that she was adopted, but had no idea that Trent was involved. I began feeling lightheaded and looked around for something to hang onto. There were a couple of Adirondack chairs on the front porch and I made my way to the nearest one. Once I sat down, I put my head between my knees, in hopes that my labored breathing would subside.

From where I was sitting, I could no longer hear their conversation. Besides, their voices had been trailing off. They sounded as if they were walking further into the house, and away from the door.

What the hell was I going to do now? My sister, Viv, was fathered by Trent. That was just insane. Mind blowing, actually. I never ever suspected anything even remotely close to this revelation.

I sat in that chair for several more minutes, contemplating the news that I had just heard. I didn't even think about how long I had been sitting there. Suddenly, the front door was yanked open and Trent stepped outside. A family of blue jays scattered. I hadn't noticed them only a few feet from where I sat.

The look on Trent's face mirrored my own. I should not have been there. I should have been long gone. I almost wish that I had been gone. But the news about Viv might actually put me one step closer to finding out my own answers.

I watched Trent, and could almost see the horrid thought that crept into his brain. His neck hairs stood on end, and his hand holding the doorknob trembled uncontrollably. The fact that I had probably overheard their conversation hit him like a brick wall.

He took short breaths before he spoke. "My god, Georgie, what are you still doing here?"

"Don't you mean to ask me if I heard your conversation right after I walked out the door?"

His face paled. He did not speak.

"Yes, I heard. All of it. I know about Viv. I'm shocked, to say the least. How could you keep that secret all of these years? How could you not tell me? And more importantly, how could you not tell Viv?"

Trent closed the door quietly behind him. Turning to me, his demeanor changed in an instant. He steeled his eyes my way. "Frankly, it's none of your business."

I flew to my feet. "How can you say that!" I said much louder than intended.

He looked toward the front door. "Keep your voice down. We don't need Beverly hearing any of this."

I lowered my voice, but not really sure why. "Why not? She already knows that Viv is yours. How long has she known?"

"I told her after Stan died."

"Why? I mean, why now? And why did you wait until after my father died? What does that have to do with anything?"

He put his palm up between us. "Whoa, hold on missy. You don't need to worry about any of that. I'm handling it."

"I would also like to know what you know about my kidnapping."

His eyes grew wide. He knew something. I could see it in his face.

"You are a lawyer. You are close to the family. You know something, don't you?" I couldn't stop my mouth. I was tired of living with all the secrets and lies. I needed answers. And I needed them immediately.

He took my by the arm and lead me, a bit forcefully I might add, to the driveway, out of sight of the front door. I struggled, but he held on tightly.

Once we reached my car, Trent stopped and leaned in so that he was only inches from my ear. "Now you listen to me. Forget what you heard. Forget all of it. If you don't, it won't end well for you. Or your family."

I yanked my arm out of his grip and stood back, looking him right in the eyes.

"Are you threatening me now? Because I'm not afraid of you." Yes I was.

"I'm just telling you the way it is. If you keep pressing this, it could be catastrophic." He raised just his left eyebrow for emphasis.

"Leave me alone," I muttered through gritted teeth.

I got in my car and drove away. My rearview mirror revealed him standing in the street, watching me until I was out of sight. Though it was a humid, summer day, I began to shiver.

CHAPTER 8

That night, I slept in fits and starts. I just could not get the conversation with my father-in-law, Trent, out of my mind. It just nagged at my brain.

Tommy and Taylor were still camping, and I was alone. Normally that's not a problem at all. But with the threats I received from Trent, I was a little on edge.

Sometime after midnight, I got out of bed to get a glass of water. I just needed a reprieve from the tossing and turning. I didn't turn on any lights as I headed toward the kitchen. I got my glass of water and sat down at the kitchen table to just decompress for a couple of minutes, before I once again attempted sleep.

Staring out the window, deep in thought, I was startled back into reality by a popping noise. It sounded like it was coming from inside the house. I stood abruptly, knocking over the wooden chair I had been sitting in. It clambered to the ground, making a lot of noise. If someone was in the house, they most certainly heard me.

Not knowing what else to do, and not being entirely sure that someone was in the house, I ducked into the living room and crawled behind the couch. It was a couple of feet from the wall, and had a table behind it. I tucked down under the table, making myself as small as I could get.

That's when I heard footsteps coming down the tiled hallway floor. No one was tiptoeing their way through. It was as if they didn't have a care in the world. It sounded like only one person, with heavy foot falls. It didn't seem as if he was trying to be stealth at all. I peered around the corner of the couch, and into the kitchen.

There was a tall man searching the kitchen with only the moonlight seeping in through the windows. He stopped at the overturned chair and stared at it for a good 20 seconds. That was an eternity, with me kneeling behind the couch. My middle aged knees ached.

Finally, he lost interest in the chair and turned toward the living room. I held my breath, as if that would make me invisible. He made a lap around the living room, passing within only a foot of my hiding space. I dared not move, not even a fraction of an inch. I just knew that if I did, he would detect any tiny little noise that I made. The house was dead silent.

Just as he turned and began heading back toward the hallway and the back bedrooms, he suddenly stopped. He slowly turned until he was facing my hiding place. It was all I could do to keep from gasping. He was actually looking straight at me. But I knew there was no way he could see me in that dark room. But then again, maybe he could. I could see him. But I was in a dark space behind the couch and he was standing in the moonlight.

He began walking straight toward me. I knew it was a risk, but I needed to scoot backwards and get out of sight just a little bit better, in the off chance that he didn't actually know I was there. Maybe I would be lucky and he hadn't really seen me. I would probably not be that lucky though.

The tall man stopped right next to where I was scrunched

down. His right hand grabbed the top of the couch and yanked, screeching it at least ten feet across the floor. I let out a yelp. I just couldn't help myself. It came out before I had a chance to even realize what I was doing. Not that it mattered anyway. He had found me.

With a gun in his left hand, he reached down with his right hand and grabbed me by the top of my head, winding his fingers in my hair. He pulled me to a standing position. I had no choice in the matter. I was going wherever the top of my head went.

Without saying a word, he dragged me across the floor and into the kitchen. And his fingers were still entangled in my hair. Though the pain was excruciating, my thoughts were more centered around how I was going to get out of my current predicament. My arms and legs were flailing in a desperate attempt at getting him to release me. It wasn't working. He had a death grip on me.

Reaching the kitchen, he finally disentangled his fingers from my hair. Then he swung his arm around, as if he were pitching a fast ball, and flung me at the counter. I hit it with such force that the wind was knocked out of me. I crumpled to the ground. I was pretty sure a rib, or three, were broken.

I didn't recognize the man. Though he was tall, he was not the same tall man who had killed me in a previous life. That man would probably be in his sixties or seventies at this point. He had probably retired from murder for hire. If that's what he actually did. What do I know though? Maybe he wanted to kill me himself, and no one else was ever involved. Except that other guy who was with him when they chased Viv and me into the cave that time. I haven't seen that guy since that fateful day.

"Get up!" It was the first thing the man had said since entering my home in the middle of the night.

I moaned. Wrapping my left arm in front of me, in order to stabilize my ribs, I used my right arm and reached up to grab the top of the counter. It took some doing, but I managed to get to my feet.

"What do you..."

"Shut up. I'll do the talking," he ordered.

Knowing that he could easily kill me, with the gun still in his hand, or even with just a swift blow, I shut my mouth immediately.

"You know I'm here to kill you, right?"

"Yeah, I figured." My words were calm, however, I was anything but. My insides were shaking so much, they were surely all jumbled up by now.

"I don't want to kill you."

Wow, that was the last thing I expected to hear from him. A killer with a conscience. Who knew?

"Then why are you here?" I had to ask. "Who sent you?"

He paced back and forth on the kitchen floor in front of me, for at least a full minute before answering.

"Well, I guess it doesn't really matter at this point if you know. I'm going to kill you soon, and you won't be able to tell anyone anyway."

I took a deep breath. "That's true. Who am I going to tell after I'm dead?"

He had no idea that it was likely I would come back. And if I did, plenty of people would be around for me to tell.

Still, he hesitated.

"What's your name?" My voice was steadier than it should have been.

I could see his face now. The back porch light had flipped on, probably in the commotion going on inside the house. He was older. Older than I was anyway. He had dark skin and jet black hair. He was a nice looking man. It made me wonder how he ended up with a horrible job like this one. Did someone have something on him? Did he just get paid really well? Was he forced into it? Those are things I would probably never know the answers to.

He turned to me. His raised eyebrows told me that no one, no victim anyway, had ever asked him his name before. I could almost see the wheels turning in his head. After a moment, he shrugged.

"Wesley."

"That's a nice name." I meant it too.

It was important to me to try to gain his confidence. Otherwise, I was absolutely going to be killed. I probably would be anyway. But I had to try. I really didn't want to die and wake up ten or more years older. At that rate, I was going to wake up at some point a very old woman.

Unfortunately, it didn't work.

"Shut up!"

It was almost as if something snapped him out of it. He came to his senses and realized where he was and what he had been sent there to do.

A lone bead of sweat made its way from my temple to my chin. I wiped it off with the back of my hand.

"I'm sorry. I just..."

"I said shut up!"

I shut up.

Before I realized what was happening, a fist slammed into my face. Stars erupted in my vision and I struggled to stay conscious. The counter was the only thing standing between me and the floor. I hung onto it for dear life. My knees threatened to give way, but I held tight. I wasn't going to go down that easily. If I did, I just knew in my heart that I would never get back up.

Wesley looked at the kitchen ceiling and laughed. Somehow, he was actually getting enjoyment out of torturing me. But I stood my ground. I shook my head in an attempt to clear the cobwebs that were threatening to take me down.

I tried again to engage him in conversation. If I was going to die, I wanted to know everything before I did. "So...you promised to tell me who sent you. And why."

Without a beat, "Did I?"

"Yes, you said it didn't matter if you told me, because the dead don't talk."

"Yeah, I guess I did."

He turned to me and I raised my eyebrows in a questioning manner.

"Okay fine. Trent. It was your father in law, Trent. He's the one that had you kidnapped as a toddler and handled your adoption. That jackass is one mean S.O.B. He told me he would kill my daughter if I didn't do this." His face fell a bit when he said that. A parent would do just about anything for their children.

By that point, I wasn't the least bit surprised. It was all coming together.

"And what about my sister, Viv? Who is her mother?" I felt that I needed to get the questions and answers as quickly as I could. I didn't know how much longer I could stay conscious. And in a standing position. My knees were weak and struggling to stay upright. Besides, that gun of his was still in his hand.

"He doesn't talk about her much. But I'm pretty sure it's Sylvia. They had a fling that didn't last long."

"Sylvia?" I needed him to tell me everything he knew.

"Yeah, I met her once. She looked like she was barely pregnant. A while later, Trent asked if I knew anyone looking to adopt. I didn't. Besides, even if I did, there was no way I was gonna get involved in that mess."

"You won't get involved in black market adoptions, but you'll kill for Trent?"

Wesley narrowed his eyes at me. That was all the warning I needed.

"Do you know where..." Oh, wait. I was just about to ask

him where I could find Sylvia. But, as far as he or I knew, I was not getting out of my kitchen alive. There would be no need for me to know where she was.

"Um, I don't remember Sylvia," I began. "Does she live around here?"

"She's was livin' over at the Highway Motel. You know, that red and white one? Or at least she was back then," he told me. "But that was so long ago. Who knows if she's even still alive."

Wesley didn't seem to know any more information about Sylvia. So I figured I would move on. He seemed to be free with the information. I guess that was because he knew he was going to kill me anyway. So it didn't matter what he told me.

"I see." Perhaps I needed a new approach. "You've never killed anyone before, have you?"

"No, but it doesn't mean that I can't." His voice was angry, and a little bit of fear showed through.

He didn't want to do this. I could see that. "Oh, of course. I know you can. But do you want to be that person? My death is going to haunt you for the rest of your life."

"Why do you think that?"

"Because you are not a killer. It's not too late to keep it that way. Don't let threats by Trent make you into a murderer. You are better than that." Was he? I didn't know.

"You don't know what you're talking about, girlie. I have to do this."

"No, you don't have to do this. I'll help you. We can go to the police and tell them everything we know. Trent will be arrested and your daughter will be safe."

"Girl, you have no idea how it works, do you?"

I really didn't.

"Trent will come after the both of us if I leave this house with you alive. People are out there watching me. We would never make it to the cops."

He walked over to the kitchen window and moved the

curtain only an inch or two. Just enough to peer out into the front yard. He must not have seen anything out of the ordinary, because he dropped the curtain. It swayed for just a moment, before coming to a rest.

Almost as if he just realized I was still standing at the counter, he turned back to me with glassy, determined eyes.

I gasped as I watched him begin to raise his gun toward me. That moment was my make it or break it moment. I had to do something. If I just stood there, I would die. That was a given. If I tried to run, I would get shot in the back. No doubt about it. Without another thought, I charged him.

CHAPTER 9

With Wesley's gun pointing right at me, he hesitated just long enough for me to spring. My ribs be damned. This was my one and only chance to save my own life and I was going to do whatever it took.

His eyes were as large as saucers as he realized I was not going to just stand there and go down easily. He didn't even have time to react. I hit the gun with one hand and somehow managed to knock the man off balance as I slammed into him. His back hit the refrigerator with some force. The gun scattered across the floor, clanking against the hard tiles the entire way. His feet went out from underneath him and he landed on the floor, hard, in a seated position. I tumbled right on top of him.

I hadn't thought past that moment. But I needed to do something, and do it fast. He would recover from the shock of it all in only a few seconds. That's all I had.

. . .

The first thing that I needed to do was get as far away from him as I could. I rolled off of his legs and pulled myself to my feet. The pain from my broken ribs was so immense, it almost brought me down.

Wesley was just beginning to come out of the shock of it all at that point. He leaned over, reaching for my legs. He managed to grab a hold of one of my ankles. Yanking on it, I lost balance and hit the floor. The back of my head made contact with the tiles. Once again, stars floated around my vision.

Before I could do anything, he crawled on top of me, setting each knee on the floor on each side of my hips. I started flailing my arms in an attempt to scratch his face, or anything at all, to protect myself. I remembered being told that if I'm ever attacked, to go for the eyes. And that's exactly what I did. I jabbed my fingers hard into his eyes. He released me and screeched in pain. But I know that I didn't do that much damage, if any at all.

While he was reacting to getting his eyes jabbed, I was trying to get him off of me. I shoved at him as hard as I could, but he wasn't budging. He was a big man, way bigger than I could handle. He certainly had the upper hand at the moment, even with the pain shooting through his eyes.

A few seconds later, the moment he recovered from my attack, I saw his fist fly back and toward my face. And then everything went dark.

PART 4

CHAPTER 1

With my arms still flailing, my eyes flew open.

The tall man was gone. I found myself sitting in the living room of Beverly and Stan. I didn't even have to think about it. I knew exactly what had happened. No moments of confusion this time. That man had killed me and I was living a new life. No doubt about it.

"Georgie, honey, are you all right? Did you fall asleep and have a bad dream?" I felt a pat on the top of my head.

I turned to Stan. He was alive again. I was thankful for that. And maybe, just maybe, I could prevent the carjacking this time. The one that had taken his life last time.

The one thing I hadn't noticed immediately was that I was looking up at Stan, though I was sitting next to him on the couch. My immediate thought was why was I sitting so much lower than him.

Until I looked down.

"Oh my god, no." I hadn't intended on saying it out loud, but it happened anyway.

"Georgie, what's the matter?" This time it was Beverly speaking.

"I uh...I gotta go to the bathroom."

I jumped up and ran toward the bathroom. I needed to look in the mirror. But then again, I really didn't need to. My legs were very small and skinny. I could see that I was very young, just from the few moments that I was on the couch.

Looking into the mirror confirmed it. In fact, I was barely tall enough to see into the mirror. My face was very young. I could not have been more than five or six years old. My hair was a bit unruly, but that was always the case with my hair.

"Well, at least I'm not an old woman." I kind of laughed to myself. It's always best to look on the bright side.

The problem was, how in the world was I going to do anything at this age. No one would ever take me seriously. I had stories to tell. I knew all about Trent and what was going on. But who would believe me? No one, that's who.

After several minutes, I heard Beverly calling to me from the living room, and I made my way back to the couch. I stood in front of the couch instead of sitting down.

"Where's Viv?" I looked around for any sign of her. She would be only two or three years old.

"Who?" Beverly asked.

Oh no. They didn't know who Viv was. That could be a problem. Oh wait. Maybe it wasn't. Could I possibly prevent Viv's kidnapping? At my age? Doubtful.

"Oh, never mind."

All three of us looked up when the doorbell rang. Not knowing what else to do with myself, I offered to answer it. My face drained of all blood when I saw who was standing at the doorway, smiling at me.

"Hi Georgie girl, come here and give your Uncle Trent a big hug."

He opened up his pudgy arms, revealing his disgusting pudgy self. I wanted nothing to do with him. And I think I did a pretty good job of making that clear. I slammed the door in his face and headed toward my bedroom. I didn't even turn when the doorbell rang again.

"Georgie! Are you going to answer the door?" It was Stanley calling from the other room.

"No!" It was all I said and I continued heading toward my room. I was a young child. I figured I could get away with some sassiness once in a while.

Less than a minute later, I heard the front door open and voices. No doubt Trent was regaling them with the story of me slamming the door in his face.

"Georgie!" It was Stan again. "Get down here!"

I huffed. Time to face the music, I guess. Though I was hoping that they would let it go, I knew in my heart that there was no way they were going to. I climbed off of my bed and started down the stairs. As soon as I saw Trent, I locked eyes with him. I did not take my eyes off of him the rest of the way down the stairs. When I reach the bottom, I walked over and stood between my parents, continuing to stare Trent down.

"Georgie, did you slam the door in Trent's face?" Beverly asked me, in a sweet voice. I'm sure she didn't believe that her cute little daughter would ever do anything so rude.

I crossed my arms in front of me. "Yes."

"Why did you do that to your Uncle Trent?"

"He's not my uncle!" I yelled. I really needed to sell the six year old attitude. And I was doing a damn fine job if you ask me.

"Well, okay, he's not technically your uncle, but Georgie, what has gotten into you?" Beverly was down on one knee in front of me by then. She wanted to look me straight in the eyes.

"He's a kidnapper." There, I said it.

"Georgie! Why would you say something like that?" Stanley interrupted.

"Because he is. He kidnapped me from my real mom." Oops, maybe I had gone too far that time. I had only been in this life for something like five minutes and was already causing trouble. Besides, Trent was a dangerous man. A little kid, such as I was, was no match for him.

"Georgie, apologize to Trent," Stan ordered.

I looked down at my feet, in the true style of a small child. "Sorry," I said, without looking up at him.

"Well, I guess that'll have to do," Stan said. "Come on in, Trent, and have a drink. Georgie, go back to your room."

Without another word I headed for the stairs again. I only went up a few steps, because I could hear the adults speaking and I wanted to know what they were saying. There was no doubt in my mind that I would be the main topic of their conversation, after my little outburst.

But, you know what? That was perfectly fine with me. Maybe it would make Stan and Beverly ask some questions. And just maybe, Trent would tell them what he knew.

"What do you think that was all about?" I heard Beverly ask. She must have assumed that I was up in my room, because she did not speak in hushed tones.

"No idea," Trent replied. "Who knows what goes on inside the heads of little girls."

"I don't even know how she knows that she was adopted. Stan and I never told her." There was a slight pause. "Right Stan?"

"Right."

"So how can she possibly know?" Beverly asked again.

"Honey," Stan began, "why are you harassing the man? He doesn't know anything."

"Well, someone knows something. Georgie is only six years old. She didn't make the story up on her own. I mean, how would she even know what kidnapping and adoption are, if we didn't explain those things to her?" Beverly asked.

"Come on, Bev, let's go sit out back and have a drink." Stan was trying to get her to leave it alone.

"No. I'm going to go talk to Georgie about it. I want to know where she came up with those crazy ideas."

I hightailed it up the stairs and leapt onto my bed, grabbing a book just in time.

Beverly walked in and sat down next to me on the bed. "Hi, sweetie, I would like to talk to you about something, okay?"

I nodded.

"Do you know what being adopted means?"

"Yes, it means that someone else had me and that now you are my parents." It was the simplest explanation I could come up with that sounded like it came from someone my age.

"Well, yes, that's right. You do know that just because you came from someone else, I'm your mom now? And I will always be your mom?"

I detected tears threatening to spill down her face.

"Yeah, I know." I nodded as I spoke. This was hurting her. I knew that. I needed to be as gentle with her as I could. I jumped up on my knees and squeezed her tightly. The tenseness in her body seemed to relax when I did that. "I love you, Mommy."

"I love you more than you'll ever know, Georgie."

I knew. There was nothing like the love between a mother and her child. Once I sat back down, she continued with the questioning.

"Do you know what kidnapping is?"

I nodded.

"What do you think kidnapping is?"

"When someone steals you from your parents."

She tilted her head my way and gave me the slightest of smiles. She was probably surprised that I knew what those terms meant.

"How do you know these things? I never told you. Your dad didn't either, did he?"

I shrugged. "No. I just know them, I guess." What else could I say?

"I see," she told me. I don't think she did. "So, who is Viv?"

"She's my little, um, she's my friend, I guess." Smooth.

"Oh, okay. It just seemed as if you expected her to be at our house tonight," Beverly explained.

"No, I just fell asleep. I don't know why I said that."

"I see." She seemed to say that a lot. "Why did you accuse your Uncle Trent of kidnapping you from your real mom?"

That was going to be a tougher one to answer.

"Because, Mommy, that's what he did." I wasn't backing down now.

"You know that's not true, honey. Why do you think that?"

How was I going to answer that one? I couldn't say anything close to, "Because in my last life, I overheard him talking and then he threatened me. And...he had me killed because of it." No, obviously that wouldn't cut it.

Think fast. Think fast. "He was talking on the phone one day about it."

With that lie, I didn't have to say who he was speaking with, because I wouldn't know.

Her eyebrows raised, involuntarily. "When was this?"

I gave her a one shouldered shrug. "I don't know. The other day."

"I see."

Did she though? Did she really believe her six year old daughter about things that I had no reason to know about? I had my doubts.

I guess that was enough for Beverly, because she got up and left my room. I fell asleep shortly thereafter. Dying and coming back multiple times could really take it out of a girl.

CHAPTER 2

Around ten the next morning, Trent showed up at our house once more. This time, Tommy was in tow.

I stopped short when Tommy walked into the living room behind his father. I smiled when I saw him. Let me tell you that six year old Tommy was just about the cutest thing I have ever seen.

"Let's go swimming!" Tommy, clad in only a pair of lime green swim trunks blew past me and out the back door before I even had a chance to respond.

As much fun as that sounded, my future husband would have to wait. I had things that I needed to do.

First on my list: Sylvia.

I needed to find out where she was, and do what I could to keep Viv from being kidnapped. Though I would miss her as a sister, she deserved to have things made right. I didn't know if Sylvia was a good person or not, and perhaps Viv would be better off in our family, but that wasn't my decision to make. I felt as if I owed it to my little sister to give her the mother who gave birth to her, and probably loved her very much.

Here was my chance. Trent was standing in the same room

with me. And Beverly. I was convinced that no matter what I said, it wouldn't go over well. But I had to try. I was six years old, for heaven's sake. It wasn't as if I could go out into the world and search things on my own.

"Where is Sylvia?" I asked Trent, point blank.

He looked at me with his mouth hanging open.

"What do you know about Sylvia?" His tone was defensive.

"I know that she has a daughter, named Viv. And that Viv is also your daughter."

Trent and Beverly were both staring at me as if I had monkeys flying out of my head.

"Georgie," Beverly jumped in. "Where are you getting all of this nonsense?"

"It's not nonsense, Mom. It's the truth. All of it." I looked Trent straight into his pudgy face. "Isn't it, Trent?"

"Well, uh, yeah, I guess she is." He was so taken aback by my questions, he seemed quite flustered. Pink splotches started creeping up from his neck.

"Georgie, what has gotten into you?" Beverly screeched. Okay, maybe it wasn't quite a screech, but close.

"I just want to make sure that Viv is okay."

"Viv?" Beverly questioned. "I thought she was a friend from school."

"She's not," I answered truthfully this time. "She's Trent's daughter and he is planning to kidnap her from her mother." I turned back to Trent. "Aren't you?"

"Georgie!" Beverly yelled. It was definitely a yell that time.

"Tell us, Trent," I added.

"You have a daughter?" Beverly asked him. "Is this really true? How do we not know about this?"

"He's embarrassed, that's why," I answered for him.

Beverly looked back up at Trent. "I see." It was her judgmental way of answering most things.

He pulled at the collar of the white dress shirt he was wearing. He was quite taken aback by getting the third degree from a six year old. Trent immediately changed the subject. "Of course I would never kidnap my own child. I don't know what you are talking about. I would never do anything like that."

I knew better.

"I want to go see her." I crossed my arms defiantly.

"Go see who?" Did Beverly really need to ask.

"Viv. That's who. And her mother. I want to see for myself that everything is as it should be." I looked to Trent for a response.

I have no idea why Trent responded the way he did, but I'll take it. "Yeah, I'll take the kid to see them. Hell, maybe she and Viv will be friends."

What? Really? That worked?

"No, Trent, you don't have to do that," Beverly told him. "Georgie is acting strangely and certainly doesn't deserve you indulging her like this."

He raised up his right palm between the two adults. "No, Bev, it's fine, really. I don't mind."

I started shaking. Suddenly I was beginning to think that going somewhere with the man would be a huge mistake.

"You can come too, Mommy." I needed the backup.

"No, you go along. I have things to do here. I'll see you in a bit." She looked at Trent. "You sure you don't mind?"

He looked down at me and I detected just the slightest upturn in the corners of his mouth. A shiver ran up my spine. "Not at all. Happy to do it. My girl here wants to make a new friend and it's no trouble at all." His eyes never left mine as he spoke.

"Um, is Tommy gonna come with us?" My eyes darted to the boy in the swimming pool.

"Of course he's going with you," Beverly answered quickly. She probably didn't like the idea of having to babysit Tommy.

"Well, yeah, he can come," Trent added.

"Great! I'll go get him." I ran for the backyard, before anyone could change their minds about our plans.

It took some doing, but I managed to coax Tommy out of the pool, with a promise of swimming together all afternoon. He dragged himself out and grabbed the nearest towel. Once he was dressed, Trent, Tommy, and I headed out.

Crawling into the backseat, it all started to hit me. I needed a plan. And I needed one fast.

CHAPTER 3

It didn't seem to take long to reach Sylvia's house. I was surprised by how close she lived to us. I wondered if, in another life, Sylvia was aware that her daughter lived so close by. It seemed likely that they could run into each other at some point. The mall, the supermarket, the gas station. The possibilities were almost endless. So why take a child from so close by? Why not take one from across the country, where the chance of running into her mother was almost nil? It seemed to me that Trent could have left his daughter with her mother, and just taken another child. But maybe there was big money in it. And maybe it was a way out of his obligation of child support. Who knows what runs through the mind of a criminal such as Trent.

I was nervous walking up the steps to the modest home. It may have been small, but it was well kept. It was easy to see that Sylvia took pride in her beautiful yellow roses that seemed to surround the house. The light green color with white trim seemed to complement the roses perfectly.

The door flew open before we even ascended the three steps to the porch.

"What the hell are you doing here?"

Sylvia was an average looking woman, probably around forty. Much too young and pretty for the likes of Trent. I looked over at him. He didn't seem the slightest bit taken aback by her outburst.

"Sylvia, we just came by to see how you and Viv are doing."

My eyes were drawn to the tiniest, and most adorable little pixie of a child peeking out around her mother's legs. When I smiled, she smiled back and pulled her head back completely behind her mother, so that I couldn't see her.

I had never known Viv to be shy. That obviously changed at some point. In a big way. The Viv I knew was smart and sassy. She took guff from no one. I loved that about her.

"Well, we are doing just fine. No thanks to you."

There was obviously no love lost between the two of them.

"What are you talking about?" Trent's voice sounded defensive. "I send you money."

She laughed out loud. "Are you talking about that measly hundred bucks you send? That doesn't even cover my latte habit."

Trent started to say something about that, when I spoke up before the three of us were sent packing.

"Hi, my name's Georgie. I told my Uncle Trent (ugh) that I wanted to meet Viv. Is that okay?" I used the best sickly sweet voice that I could muster.

Sylvia look down at me, as if she had just noticed me for the first time.

"And who are you?"

That's how someone talks to a six year old?

"I'm, um..." How to answer that one? I wasn't actually related to Trent. "I'm..."

Trent jumped in. "She's my niece, that's who she is. She wants to meet her little cousin. I said it was okay. You gotta problem with that?" He widened his stance and gave her a glare that dared her to argue with him.

"Mommy, please?" It was Viv's little pixie voice.

Sylvia looked down at her daughter. She smiled as she rubbed the top of the girl's head. "Sure, honey, it's fine with me."

"Yay!" Viv ran down the steps and straight at me. She took my hand and pulled me toward the house. "Come on, I'll show you my bedroom."

Now that was the Viv I knew and loved.

I turned to see Tommy following us inside. Oh yeah, I had almost forgotten about him. Off in the distance, I could hear Trent and Sylvia talking. Well, arguing was more like it. I couldn't quite make out what they were saying.

Viv gave us a detailed tour of her room, though it was no more than ten by ten feet. It was pink and white, with frilly lace white curtains. Perfect for a three year old. Tommy and I just smiled at each other as she told us the names of every single one of her stuffed animals. And there were a lot of them.

I turned to see Sylvia standing in the doorway, leaning on the frame, watching us with a smile. I had the feeling that Viv didn't get many visitors and that Sylvia was grateful for our presence.

"Hey guys, how's it going in here?" she asked.

"We are having so much fun, Mommy. Georgie and Tommy are my new best friends."

I couldn't help but laugh at her young innocence. Tommy and Sylvia joined in. Viv didn't seem to notice.

"Would you kids like some lemonade?"

This was my chance. "Can I help you get it?"

"Sure. What was your name again?"

"Georgie."

"Okay, Georgie. Follow me."

I followed her down the short hallway and into the kitchen. "Where's Trent?"

"Oh, he's outside on the phone. He's always on that damn, um, on that phone." She didn't quite catch herself in time.

She fished three plastic cups from the cupboard and set them down on the counter in front of me. I spoke while we had a few minutes alone.

"Oh, I was wondering if I could talk to you about something?"

Sylvia turned to me just as her hand landed on the refrigerator door. Her face was lit up with amusement. It was kind of a grown up phrase. She probably wondered what I could possibly want to talk to her about.

"Sure, honey. What is it?"

"I need to say this fast, so please listen to me. I know I'm only six years old, but I know things. Please take what I say seriously." I didn't have time to figure out how to sound like a six year old. I needed to get it out, and fast.

She let go of the refrigerator door and turned to face me. "Okay."

"Trent is a bad guy."

She laughed. "Yeah, don't I know it."

I put my hand up in the air between us, in a stopping motion. I kept my voice low. "No, please listen. He is planning to kidnap your daughter and sell her into the black market." I turned toward the front door, but there was no sign of Trent.

"Oh honey, I'm sure that's not true. She is Trent's daughter also, and he loves her. At least I think he does. And do you even know what the black market is?"

"I know what all of it is. This is not a joke. You need to keep Viv with you at all times. Trent is an adoption attorney, and this is how he makes most of his money. Black market babies are big money. Viv is not safe." I widened my eyes for emphasis.

"Oh Georgie, how would you know any of this?" I could tell she didn't believe me.

"I..." How to answer that? "I overheard it all. Please, just move out of here. Go far away. If you don't, Trent will send someone to take her. Once she's adopted into another family, you will never see her again. This is really serious."

It wasn't completely lost on me that I probably sounded like a ridiculous little child who didn't know what she was talking about. But I somehow needed to get my point across and make sure that she took me seriously. I just wasn't fully aware of how to do that.

The front door opened wide and Trent stepped into the living room. "Hi girls, what do you two have your head together about?"

"Who were you talking to on the phone, Trent?" I don't know if Sylvia actually believed what I was telling her, but she did sound suspicious of Trent.

He looked at her with a slight grin. "Do I have to answer to you now?"

"Just answer the question, Trent."

"Well, if you must know, I was speaking with Georgie's father. We had some business to discuss."

My father? I gasped. It was as if a lightbulb actually flashed over my head. Oh my god. Stan. He was involved in this whole thing. What other business could they possibly have together? It all made sense. That's why he and Beverly ended up with two adopted children, who were kidnapped. Stan was in on it all along. I was still pretty sure that Beverly had no clue. I couldn't imagine her going along with a felony that could land all of them in prison for a very long time.

Sylvia knelt down in front of me. "Georgie, are you all right?"

I had been holding my breath and was probably a little pale as a result. I took deep breaths to resume my normal breathing. Turning to Trent, I couldn't help but stare.

"Uh huh, I'm fine." I didn't take my eyes off of Trent.

Trent looked up at Sylvia. "You going to be home later? I'm going to send someone over with a...gift for you."

Sylvia was still on her knees in front of me. Her eyes bore into mine. Somehow, some way, she was starting to possibly believe what I was telling her.

She stood up and turned to Trent. "A gift?"

"Yeah. Just a little something for you. A treat, you know?"

"Hmm, really? Do you want to see Viv while you are here?"

Trent didn't hesitate. "No, she's having fun with the kids. I'll have plenty of opportunity to see her later."

Will you? No, I didn't actually say it out loud.

"You know, I'm suddenly not feeling all that well. Maybe you all should go home. I'd like to lie down." Sylvia rubbed her forehead for emphasis.

"Yeah, okay," Trent responded. "But you'll be home later today, right?"

He seemed awfully invested in making sure she was going to be home. I had a really bad feeling about what was going to happen that afternoon.

"I'll go get Tommy," I volunteered. I just needed to get out of that room.

The entire ride home, I contemplated what I had told Sylvia. I didn't even know for sure if kidnapping Viv was a plan of Trent's in this lifetime. Things could totally be different. Maybe he was planning to go over and propose to her. I laughed and the other occupants of the car looked over at me. No, I didn't think that was possible. Trent was a bad guy. He was planning Viv's kidnapping, and I knew it.

And probably the worst thing of all? My own father, Stan, was involved. I just knew he was. It all made sense. It all was coming together.

Now...what do I do about it all?

Once again, I was only six years old. This was not an ideal situation.

CHAPTER 4

Late that very night, I tossed and turned in bed. There was no way that I was getting any sleep that night. All I could think of was what Trent had said to Sylvia. He had asked her, more than once, whether she was going to be home the rest of the day. Why would he be so concerned about her plans, if he didn't have something up his sleeve? He was up to no good, and I knew it.

Very late that night, or early that morning was more like it, I heard the doorbell ring and excited voices. Yeah, something was definitely up. And if I had a million dollars I would have bet that it had something to do with Trent.

I climbed out of bed and wrapped my lavender robe around my tiny body. Tiptoeing down the stairs, I stopped about four steps down, so that I could sit and listen to the adults, without detection.

"Yeah, it was a real blood bath," Trent told my parents.

A blood bath? I had missed the part about what happened.

"And who is this little one?" I heard Beverly ask.

"This is my daughter, Viv."

Viv was crying. Whatever this blood bath was, surely traumatized the poor kid.

"Well, hi Viv. You remember my daughter, Georgie, right?"

"Yeah," Viv said in the tiniest little voice. "She's my best friend."

"Perfect. Would you like to go up to her room and sleep with her tonight?" Beverly offered. "If that's okay with you, Trent?"

"That's perfect. I was hoping that the two of you could watch her for me for a little while. The police want to question me, and are outside waiting for me."

"Oh, of course," Beverly told him. She didn't even wait for Stan to chime in. "Come on, Viv, I'll take you to her room."

I leapt to my feet and headed down the stairs. "I'll show her."

"Georgie, what are you doing up?" Stan asked.

"Um, you guys are making a lot of noise. You woke me." It was mostly true.

"Hi Georgie," Viv squealed, taking my hand. She managed to smile, even though her face was red and streaked from crying.

Once in my room, I got her all tucked in and told her I would be right back. I then sneaked back down the stairs to see if I could find out anything further.

"So she had a gun?" Beverly asked.

"Yeah, I didn't even know Sylvia owned one," Trent replied. "But when the burglars, or whoever they were, broke into her house, she started firing. At least that's what the cops said. And they fired back. Everyone was killed. Thank god, Viv was in her room and was unharmed."

Holy moly. So Trent did send his thugs over to Sylvia's house. And they killed her. My warnings to her probably caused her to be on alert. She was still killed, but maybe she saved Viv from being hurt also. Or at least saved her from being kidnapped.

But now Viv was here with us. So did I even change anything? No, she wasn't kidnapped, but her mother was murdered. I had a feeling that Viv would be staying with us for good.

There was nothing I could do that night, so I slowly walked back up the stairs and to my room. I climbed into bed next to Viv, letting her snuggle up with me. She needed someone to be there for her. I don't know how much she saw, but clearly she saw or heard something. Otherwise why would she be so upset and crying?

I drifted off to sleep just as the sun began to brighten my room. It didn't matter. I was exhausted by then.

CHAPTER 5

I found myself running. It was dark and cold. Was I dreaming? It felt like I had just been slugged in the face. Hard. Was I unconscious?

I shivered and looked down at myself. Nope, not a dream. I was older now, no longer a tiny six year old. I had no idea how I died, but obviously I did. Or perhaps, I just fell asleep and woke up older, not remembering anything in between. It had happened before.

Either way, here I was. Once again in the forest.

My feet were bare and bleeding. The whole scenario was strangely familiar. Then it hit me. A few lifetimes ago, I had found myself in this exact predicament. In the forest, in the middle of the night, barefoot and shivering from the cold. That was the time that I fell into the sinkhole, or possibly one of its offshoots, because I couldn't see three feet in front of me.

This night was exactly like that. I was even wearing the same clothing. Was it possible that I was reliving that exact night? The thought horrified me. What if I was in some sort of endless loop? Going around and around, living the same lives over and over, and never finding an end to them? If that was the case, then I was 18 years old once again. Better than six I surmised.

Tears flowed freely down my face. I wiped them away with the back of my hand. My face felt gritty to the touch. A low growl resonated all around me, somewhere in the dark. I stopped walking and stood perfectly still, trying to get my bearings. I needed to know where that growl was coming from. It was impossible to tell.

The growl again. This time more intense. I drew in a quick breath and scanned the forest with only my eyes, not moving a muscle. Still, I could not find the source of the sound. If I had to venture a guess, I would say it was a wolf.

Did I dare continue walking? Should I just stand my ground, hoping he would bore of me and move along? That seemed unlikely. I felt that my only choice was to keep walking and try my best to get out of the forest. Maybe I would reach the edge and out into a clearing before the wolf caught up to me.

Then, even worse than the sound of the wolf, a thought flashed through my mind. Someone else was in the forest. But who? I wasn't sure. Even though I couldn't hear anyone, I knew they were there. I needed to get away. I couldn't let him catch me.

I quickened my pace and picked my way through the dense brush, wincing each and every time I took a step. Bare feet, pine cones, and rocks did not mix. I could feel the cuts and bleeding with every step.

The growl came once again. This time, it sounded as if it was only a few feet in front of me. I stopped, holding my breath. The moment I did, the ground in front of me seemed to be giving way. My feet were sliding forward as dirt and rocks fell. Was I on the edge of a ravine? My eyes were beginning to adjust to the darkness. I could barely make out the area where the ground gave way. It seemed to be some sort of...oh no.

The sinkhole. I was standing right at the edge of the sinkhole. If it hadn't been for the growl of the wolf, or whatever creature it was, I would surely have fallen in. My life would be over now. Once again.

I didn't have time to wonder whether the wolf was stalking me or warning me. It wasn't important. I backed up quickly, for fear that I was going in next.

Since I was almost certain that I was at the sinkhole, I knew where I was. I had been there a few times and knew my way around a bit. I walked around it to get my bearings. I found the large rock that was just to the right of the sinkhole as you came up the path from town. I almost collapsed with relief. I knew how to get out of the forest.

I turned toward the path, and toward town, and headed out. It still took me over an hour to get to the road. Bare feet were not conducive to a quick retreat. Thankfully, I never heard that bone chilling growl again. And whoever was following me through the forest, if anyone actually was, never caught up to me. Perhaps he was having just as hard a time making his way through the trees as I was.

Once I hit the road, I hesitated for only the merest of seconds. I knew where I needed to go. I turned to my left and broke into a sprint. Be damned my aching and bleeding feet.

CHAPTER 6

Arriving at Ivy's house, I stopped on the sidewalk to catch my breath. I hadn't slowed down for even a second on the run from the forest. Bending over, hands on knees, it took at least a full minute before my breathing and beating heart slowed down enough for me to actually get my nerve up enough to approach the front door. It was the middle of the night after all. And I hadn't seen or talked to Ivy in a couple of lifetimes. Would she recognize me? Only one way to find out.

I walked up to the front door and rang the door bell before I lost my nerve. A light upstairs flicked on, then I could see the stair light come on through the curtains of the front windows.

"Who is it?" It was Ivy's voice.

Thank god, she was alive this time. "Um, it's...it's Georgie." How else was I to answer?

There was a long pause on the other side of the door. I can only imagine what was running through her mind. Finally, the door cracked open just a tiny bit. I could see one eye through the opening between the door and the frame.

The door flew open wide and Ivy stood there looking at me. She scanned me from head to toe. Still, she said nothing. I followed her gaze down the walkway, leading to the sidewalk and road. I drew in a quick breath when I realized what it was she was looking at. My footprints. My bloody footprints.

I turned back to her and she was looking down at my feet. They were bruised and cut. That's when I realized that I must have looked a fright. I'm sure my hair was all tangled, and I had cuts from head to toe. What must Ivy think of me?

"Um, I was being chased through the forest."

Ignoring my comment, "You are Georgie, aren't you?" It was the first thing she had said to me.

I wrapped my arms around in front of myself in an effort to stave off the chilly night. "Yes, I really am."

She noticed my gesture and stood back to allow enough room for me to enter. "Come in out of the cold."

This time was different. She didn't grab me in a big hug. She didn't start blubbering all over me. Why was this time different? Did something happen that I was unaware of? Either way, I was grateful and walked into the house. I stood my ground in the foyer though. There was no way I was going to walk across her pretty carpet with my bloody feet.

She noticed what I was doing. "Oh, let me get you a wet towel for those feet. You poor girl." She ran into the living room and came right back with a blanket. "Here, wrap this around you while I go get that towel. You must be freezing."

She returned a couple of minutes later with the towel, a chair, and a some bandages . She pulled the chair right up to me and told me to sit. Then she commenced cleaning off my bloody feet, drying them, and wrapping them in bandages. Neither one of us said a word while she worked.

Once done, she reached out her hand for mine. "Now come on, I'll make you some hot tea and we can talk."

"Can I use the bathroom?"

"Oh, of course. It's right down there, first door on your right." She pointed down the hall as she kept walking.

My reflection in the mirror was frightening, to say the least. I was disheveled, had dirt streaked on my face, and scratches all over me. I must have fallen multiple times for that to all have happened. What Ivy must be thinking!

I took a few minutes and cleaned myself up as best I could. My blouse had spots, large spots, of blood dried on it. There was nothing I could do about that.

I turned at the knock on the door. "Georgie? I have a clean t-shirt here and some sweatpants and socks, if you would like to change. I'll leave them right outside the door."

"Thanks, that would be great."

Ivy probably had no idea how grateful I was for the fresh clothing. They were a little baggy, but I didn't care. I felt so much better after cleaning up and changing.

There was a brush on the counter, but I didn't dare use it. Who uses someone else's hairbrush? So, I ran my fingers through my hair in a desperate attempt at taming my wild locks. It worked fairly well. By the time I was done and dressed, I looked almost human again.

I made my way to the kitchen table and I sat while Ivy was finishing up her tea making. She chatted about her dog and what she did that day, while she worked. Not a word about who I was or what I was doing there. I found that very odd. But maybe she was processing the whole thing. Maybe she just needed a minute to really get the reality of my presence.

"Here you go, dear." Ivy set the cup of steaming tea in front of me and took a seat at the table. "Would you like sugar or honey for your tea?"

I shook my head.

She took in my hair and clothing from head to toe without moving at all. Looking back up into my eyes, she smiled. "You look much better. How do you feel?"

I nodded. "Definitely much better. Thank you." I took a sip.

"How's your tea?"

I couldn't stand the small talk any longer. "Why aren't you acting like it's strange that I'm here? I mean, I was kidnapped from you so long ago, and you don't seem to care." I blurted it all out without thinking. I seemed to do that a lot.

Though she gave me a slight smile, her eyes were sad. "Oh, that's not it at all. I'm just...cautious. Optimistically cautious, I guess. You've been here before. Did you know that? Do you remember that?"

"No...I mean, yes, I remember coming to you before, when I was a teenager. But how do you remember?"

"It was in this lifetime. You were about 15 years old. You came to me. You spoke with me and Jack and Harper. Do you remember that?"

I nodded, completely in shock, I'm sure.

"Then you took off. When you came back about two weeks later, your sister, Viv went missing. Do you remember me speeding through the streets, trying to get you home?"

"Yes, oh my god. And then we had a car accident. I thought I died." I'm sure my mouth was hanging open at that point.

"No, you didn't die. But you were in a coma for a couple of weeks. You don't remember waking up from that?"

"No, not at all. After that car accident, I woke up almost immediately as an adult, with a husband and a young son. I don't remember anything at all from this life after the accident. Have we seen each other since then?"

"Just once. I went to the hospital after you woke up and you didn't know who I was. I don't know if that was a temporary condition from your head injury or not. But, as strange as it sounds, I decided to leave you alone. Your parents were there and I could see that they loved you very much. I didn't want to get in the middle of all that."

"And you didn't think to call the police?" It wasn't an accusation. Just an honest question.

"I did think about it. But I never did. I just wanted to do the right thing by you. You seemed happy with them. And you have never contacted me since. So I figured you never regained your memory of me."

"I had no idea that happened. I don't remember anything between that accident and today."

"Well, there's nothing we can do about that. You are here now and that's all that matters."

Startled, both of us looked to the windows when a gush of wind blew a tree branch into the window hard. I completely expected it to shatter the window, but it didn't.

CHAPTER 7

Ivy and I sat there for the next two hours talking about almost everything. She told me all about my brother and sister, Jack and Harper, and what they were doing now. Jack was married, with a young son of his own. Harper was in college. I couldn't wait to get to know them better.

All the while, the weather was getting worse and worse. The wind and thunder shook the house causing us to worry.

I told her all about my kidnapping and how Trent was behind it. I also told her that my father, Stan was involved. But I was positive that Beverly knew nothing at all.

She smiled when I told her about my six year old self going to Sylvia and warning her of the impending kidnapping of her daughter, Viv. And how Sylvia got her gun and protected Viv... at the expense of her own life.

"What?" I asked, because she was still smiling.

"Oh, I'm just so proud of you. What other six year old would have the nerve to go to a perfect stranger and convince her that you knew her daughter was going to get kidnapped? I mean, it's unheard of."

"Well, I suppose," I responded. "But, even though my body

was six, I was much older in my mind. So I really wasn't a brave child. Not really anyway."

"Perhaps not. But think about it from Sylvia's perspective. To her, you actually were a small child. You managed to convince her, even though most adults probably would have brushed your comments to the side, thinking you had an active imagination. There's nothing trivial about that."

"Yeah, I guess you are right." I smiled at my own accomplishment.

A thunderous boom, which knocked a framed photo off of the kitchen wall, hit the house and we both jumped to our feet in reaction. Sitting back down, we laughed.

"You are going to spend the night tonight, right?" Ivy asked. It didn't seem like a question to me. More like a statement of fact.

I nodded. "Yes, I guess I should. I don't want to go back out in this. But, I should call my...Beverly, to make sure she isn't worried about me."

"Oh, of course. I'll get us some more tea while you call her." Ivy picked up my cup and headed to the stove.

"Hi Mom." I side eyed Ivy to see her reaction to me calling someone else 'Mom.' She turned her back to me. I couldn't quite tell if that was on purpose or not. I didn't want to hurt her feelings, but I did have another mother.

"Georgie! Where have you been? We've been worried sick!" Beverly's voice was a little bit frantic.

"Oh, I'm sorry. I'm just over at a friend's house. Trying to keep out of the weather, you know?"

"Okay, that's fine. I'm glad you are all right. Do you want me to come pick you up?"

I shook my head, as if she could see me through the phone. "No. I'm going to stay the night. There is no need for you to go out in this. It's really bad out there."

"Yeah, okay. That's probably a good idea."

I was almost afraid to ask the next question, but I needed to know what happened to Viv in this lifetime. "Is..." I hesitated. "Is Viv there?"

I watched the sliding door as the rain pelted it. I kind of liked it.

"Yes, she's here. She's right in front of me, eating ice cream. In this weather. Can you imagine?"

Oh thank goodness. Viv was living with Beverly. That was fantastic news. I mean, maybe she would be better off with her mother, Sylvia, but I didn't know where Sylvia was or if she was even still alive in this lifetime. I was just glad that she was somewhere safe.

Out of nowhere, I heard a loud crashing sound. I spun around in the kitchen, fully expecting a tree branch to be in the middle of the room with shattered glass everywhere. But there was nothing, that's when I realized that the sound had come from the telephone.

A scream screeched through the receiver.

"Mom, are you all right?"

"Hold on."

I heard the telephone clank on the kitchen counter as she laid it down. Or dropped it was more likely. I paced the kitchen floor waiting for her to return.

"What's going on?" Ivy asked me. She was watching my every move.

I put my hand over the phone to muffle our conversation from Beverly. "I don't know." Tears were filling my eyes. "I heard a crash and someone scream. I think it was Viv."

Ivy put down what she was doing and walked over, wrapping her arms around me. I laid my head on her shoulder. But that didn't last long. I was almost frantic. I didn't know what had happened over at my house and I needed to find out. Someone needed to get back on the phone. And quickly.

"Georgie, are you still there?" It was Beverly.

"Yes, I'm here. What happened?"

"A branch crashed into the window. It hit Viv, cutting her leg pretty badly. She's bleeding and will need stitches. I need to get her to the hospital."

"Okay, call me as soon as you get there," I told her. I gave her Ivy's phone number.

Three minutes later, Beverly called me back. "My car won't start!" she wailed into the phone. I could hear the panic in her voice. "I can't get the bleeding to stop!"

"Okay, Mom, don't panic. I'm coming. Just wait there for me." I hung up the phone in a panic.

I turned to Ivy. "Can I borrow your car? Please?" I'm sure the look on my face told her everything that she needed to know and she agreed readily.

"Of course. Here." She fished her car keys from her purse. "Take them. Call me when you know more, okay?"

"I will." I couldn't hold back the tears at that point, and let loose a flood of them.

Ivy hugged me once again. "She'll be fine. I promise." When she let me go, Ivy eyed what I was wearing. "Well, what you are wearing will have to do. But you do need some shoes. You can't go out in this weather in only socks. You look about my size. Hang on."

Ivy returned a couple of minutes later with a pair of baby blue sneakers. They were a bit snug, but they would do. I tore out of the house like my feet were on fire. I heard Ivy calling after me to call her with any news. I promised I would.

The storm was the worst I had ever seen. There was no moon, and therefore, it was about as dark as I had ever seen it. The clouds and the rain, blocked out all of the little bit of light we might have gotten from the stars.

Even the car's headlights did very little to help pierce through the gloom of the night. The trees were swaying so far from their sturdy base that I thought one of them might very well uproot and land on the hood of my car.

Something very loud and heavy banged into the passenger side of the car, causing me to jump and temporarily lose control. The car began to skid across the slippery roadway and straight toward a swaying palm tree. I hit the brakes out of instinct, knowing that was not the right thing to do. But I couldn't help myself. That tree was coming at me quicker than it should have.

Ivy's car slammed into the tree, drivers side door first. I felt the crushing blow, slamming the left side of my head into the door window. As we came to an abrupt stop, I was thrown the other way. I felt as if I was being jostled around like I was a player in some video game.

Suddenly, everything went quiet. All I could hear was the drumming of the rain on the windshield, and the windshield wipers still doing their best to clear it away.

I sat there, a bit stunned, for probably a full five minutes. That doesn't sound like much time, but when you are stunned and bleeding from a car accident, it can feel like an eternity. When I finally got my wits back about me, I started the car back up, thankfully it started easily, and headed back toward my house.

I made it the rest of the way without incident, though I was a nervous wreck by the time I got there. Driving in such darkness and with the pelting rain and wind, it was just difficult to see where I was going. And it was taking a lot longer than it should have. But if I didn't get there in one piece, I was going to do Viv no good.

I pulled into the driveway behind a black SUV that I did not recognize. I wondered who was there and why they didn't take my little sister to the hospital. Running into the house, soaking from head to toe, I found my mother and sister in the living room. Also, standing a few feet away, watching my mother trying to stop the bleeding from Viv's leg, was none other than Trent.

"Georgie, you are finally here!" Beverly exclaimed.

I turned to Trent. "Why didn't you take her to the hospital?" My tone was not cordial.

"Hey, I just got here." His tone was defensive.

"Whatever." I suppressed the desire to roll my eyes his way. I turned to Viv. "How bad is it?"

"I'm dying, Georgie!" 15 year old Viv wailed at me.

"Oh don't be so dramatic," Trent admonished.

That time I did not suppress my eye rolling. This was the first time I had seen Trent in this lifetime, and I was already tired of him. I don't know why he even needed to be there at the house anyway. I knew that Viv was his daughter. But no one else knew. So why did they think he was there?

I looked around. "Where's Dad?"

"He's out of town at a conference for work," Beverly responded. "I called him, but he didn't answer. He's probably in the middle of a meeting."

"Oh," I replied. "Come on, I'm taking you to the hospital." I reached for Viv's arm.

"No you aren't."

I turned to Trent. "Excuse me?"

"I said that you are not taking my...er...Viv to the hospital."

Nice catch, I thought. He almost called her his daughter in front of her. Now that would have been a mess.

"Yes I am." I pushed past his enormous girth. He seemed to get bigger and bigger in each of my lifetimes. "Come on Viv."

Trent grabbed my arm and shoved me backward. Tripping over the ottoman in the middle of the floor, I righted myself just in time. I stood my ground.

"What the hell is wrong with you?" I asked him. "She needs to go to the hospital."

"You have blood oozing down the side of your head," Trent

informed me. "You don't look like you are in shape to take anyone anywhere."

I reached up my left hand and felt the sticky wet side of my head. My hair was dripping in blood and rainwater. I must have been a sight to see.

"What? This?" I held out my bloody hand. "It's nothing. Just a minor fender bender on the way over. I'm fine." It wasn't minor, but that was something I could deal with later. At the moment, I needed to help my sister.

"Well, that's great and all, but you still aren't taking her," Trent informed me again.

Trent grabbed my arm again and pulled me so that his lips were only an inch or so from my ear. "If you go near her, I'll kill you," he whispered, so that no one else in the room could hear.

I looked over at Beverly, who seemed completely preoccupied with Viv and hadn't said anything about our scuffle. Had she even noticed?

Beverly finally spoke up. "Look, I don't know what is the problem between you two, and right now I don't care." She looked me straight in the eyes. "Georgie, I want you to take Viv. I need to stay here and try to get a hold of your father. Once I do, then Trent and I will follow you to the hospital."

"I'm not staying here," Trent jumped in. "I'm going with them."

Beverly slid her eyes over to Trent. "You know what? I don't even care right now. I just want her to get taken care of. Thankfully, the bleeding has almost stopped. But she still needs to be seen by a doctor. You two go." She flicked her wrist at us dismissively. "Take Viv and I will get a taxi after I've talked to your father. Okay?" She looked back and forth between me and Trent. Her tone said she was not in the mood for any guff from us.

We both nodded. "Yeah, okay," we both said in unison.

CHAPTER 8

Piling into Ivy's car, I made Trent sit in the front seat with me, though I was not happy about it. I wanted Viv to lie down in the back seat. Beverly brought a pillow and covered Viv up with a blanket for the ride.

"Please take care of my baby. I'll be at the hospital very soon, I promise."

With that, the three of us headed out for the ten minute ride to the hospital.

I peeked over the seat to my little sister, lying there so still. She didn't seem to be bleeding anymore, but she was pale. I didn't know if that was from lack of blood or not. It seemed like it probably was. Her eyes were closed and she seemed to be resting.

"So what is your problem with me?" I whispered to Trent in the seat next to me.

"You know what my problem is!" he spat out.

"I...don't remember."

It sounded like something had happened between the two of us during the time that I didn't remember, after the accident with Ivy. Whatever it was, I could tell that the man hated me. In my previous lives, he doted on me. He called me his baby girl. That was certainly not the case in this lifetime.

Trent gave me an incredulous stare. "Is this a joke?"

"No. I...uh...I hit my head in the car accident." Ooo, good one, I thought. "I'm feeling a little confused about a few things. So, why don't you enlighten me?"

Would that actually work?

It would. It did.

"You're a pain in the ass. You know that?" Trent wasn't holding his feelings back. That was for sure.

"I've been called worse." I held back a smile. I don't even know why. I wasn't enjoying the conversation at all.

"Whoa, watch out!" Trent yelled. "There, in the road!"

I swerved to avoid the trash can rolling across the road. The car slid a bit, but I didn't lose control this time.

"I saw it," I told him. "You don't have to yell."

"You are gonna get us killed." He grabbed onto the dashboard for emphasis. I glanced over and ignored his dramatic gesture.

"So...are you going to tell me what the problem is between the two of us or not?" I prodded. "You started with me being a pain in the ass."

He shook his head. "Yeah, I remember. And you are. The problem is that you have been accusing me for weeks of being a kidnapper. And a murderer. Of course, you don't have any proof of any of it, which is why no one has locked me up. And they won't. Because I didn't do any of that."

"The hell you didn't!" I was the one yelling that time. "You might not have kidnapped me personally, but I know for a fact that you are behind the whole thing."

"Georgie!"

"Oh shiiiiiit!"

Something flew out of the darkness and hit the windshield of the car, hard, cracking it into a spider web like design. If my vision in the rainy night was bad before, it was almost non-existent at that point.

I pulled over to gather my wits about me. I was a nervous wreck.

"What's going on?" It was a sleepy voice from the back seat.

"Your sister is trying to kill us, that's what's going on." Trent answered before I could.

"I'm not trying to kill us. I'm trying to get Viv to the hospital. I don't know why you needed to come along anyway!" I screeched at him.

Before I realized what was going on, Trent reared his arm back and slugged me in the face. I saw stars, but I managed to keep conscious. I didn't even think about what was going to happen next. Instinctively I guess, I yanked off my seatbelt and flung at him. I hit him with everything I had. That man had made my life, my lives actually, miserable. And I had just had enough.

The fight was on.

The two of us struggled in the front seat for what seemed like an eternity. When Trent wrapped his hands around my throat, I knew I was in trouble. He was much larger than I was and I didn't have a chance to protect myself against him. Not really anyway.

"Georgie!" Viv screamed from the back seat.

I tried to answer her, but only a gurgle came out. I couldn't breathe and my vision began to fade. Suddenly, Trent released my throat and I struggled to breathe, my full vision began returning. My airway felt like it was collapsing and it was going to take a while to open back up. I didn't know if I was going to stay conscious long enough for that to happen.

I watched in shock and awe as Trent screamed and fell limp against the dashboard of the car. He was still alive and awake, but barely. Did he have a heart attack? I didn't know what happened.

"I'm sorry," Viv cried. "I didn't know what else to do."

I looked at her with my eyebrows scrunched together. "What do you mean..."

My voice trailed off the moment I saw it. The knife. It was protruding out of Trent's back. Viv looked scared to death, as if she might collapse at any moment. She was pale and gasping for breath.

"Oh my god, Viv, are you all right?" I reached over the back seat and hugged her the best I could, given our positions in the car.

"I...uh...yeah. I guess," she murmured. "Is he...dead?"

We both looked at Trent. I put my hand on his back, because he was hunched over. "He's still breathing. But there's a lot of blood. We need to get to the hospital. Now. How is your leg?"

She looked down at it. "It's okay. I'm not bleeding anymore."

"Okay, put your seatbelt back on," I ordered. "We need to get moving, before he bleeds to death."

As I reached for my seatbelt, Trent made what sounded like a guttural growl. He lunged for me. The knife was still sticking out of his back.

With as much blood as he had lost, and I'm sure he was in a weakened state, he still was able to overpower me. With his hands once again around my throat, I struggled to breathe.

"Georgie!" I heard Viv cry out.

Seconds later, the car door that I was leaning against flew open, and I landed with a thud on the muddy ground just outside. Within seconds, I was soaking wet and freezing.

"Georgie, get up!" It was Viv kneeling next to me, grabbing my arm and trying to get me to stand.

I glanced up at her through the pouring rain. Her hair was a soggy, stringy mess. Though I was still trying to get my breathing back to normal, after Trent let go of my throat, I was more concerned for Viv at that moment.

"Are you okay? How's your leg?" I croaked out with a raspy voice.

"My leg is fine. I'll live." Viv sounded irritated with me. I don't know why. I was the one lying on the side of the road in the freezing rain. "You're the one I'm worried about."

"Is he...dead this time?" My eyes averted from Viv over to Trent. He was lying across the front seats, with his head hanging over the edge of the seat and right above where I was sitting in the mud.

"No, he's not dead." She glanced over at him. "At least I don't think so. Get up, Georgie. We need to get out of here, before Trent wakes up. If he wakes up," she ordered.

I let Viv help me to my feet. Against my better judgment, I reached over and put my fingers against Trent's flabby neck. It took some doing, but I managed to find a pulse.

"He's alive," I announced.

"Fantastic." Viv's voice was dripping with sarcasm. "Come on, let's go."

I tilted my head at her, and brushed the soggy hair from my face. "Where are we going? The car is here."

"I don't know." Clearly, she hadn't thought any of it through. She looked over at Trent again. "Let's pull him out of the car. Then we can take it."

"And leave him on the side of the road? In this storm?" I asked. "He'll die."

"Yeah, so?" That didn't sound like Viv at all. "Look," she continued, "the man tried to kill you. Why do you care what happens to him?" She was yelling over the storm.

She kind of had a point, and I hesitated for a moment. The man was responsible for my kidnapping, and for my death, more than once. But I really wasn't the type of person to just leave and let someone die on the side of the road, in the mud and storm. Even if he was a kidnapper and murderer. I just couldn't do it. He could go to prison instead. I was fine with making that happen.

I yelled back. The thunder was overwhelming. "I understand what type of person he is, but we can't just leave him here to die. I couldn't live with myself if I did that."

We both ducked when a massive lightning bolt hit close by.

"Come on," I ordered. "Help me get him back to his seat. We can take him to the hospital."

Viv let out a huff. "Okay, fine. I'll help, but I don't have to like it."

"I'll run around to the passenger side. Hang on!" I shivered as I made my way around the car. Pulling open the passenger door, I climbed up on the floor of the car and grabbed onto Trent's shirt. "You push, and I'll pull," I told Viv.

"Wait just a second." Viv reached over and yanked the knife out of Trent's back, flinging it into the backseat floorboard.

I just shook my head at the carefree way she went about it. It was as if she were pulling a knife from a Thanksgiving turkey.

It was quite a struggle, and took us several minutes, but the two of us managed to get him sitting upright. Trent was still unconscious, and the seat was covered in blood. Great, Ivy is going to love this, I thought. I pulled the seatbelt across his girth and had Viv connect it on her side of him.

Once we were all situated back in our respective seats, we were on our way once again.

Not a mile down the road, Trent regained consciousness. Before I realized what he was doing, he grabbed the steering wheel and jerked it, causing us to skid across the roadway, and right toward the lake. Red Lake was only a few feet off of the road, off a short cliff, and was whipping around wildly in the storm.

"Oh my god!" Viv yelled from the backseat as we watched the lake rushing toward us. It all seemed like it was happening in slow motion.

It was if we had hit a huge patch of ice, and were just sliding across it. No matter what I did, I could not control the car. The driver's side of the car hit the lake with a huge jolt. Though we had our seatbelts on, all three of us were thrown to the side, straining against the seatbelts.

For a moment, I thought the car might roll, but it fell back down onto all four wheels. Within seconds, the car began to sink.

CHAPTER 9

"Georgie, help me. My seat belt is stuck!" Regardless of the words she said, I could hear the panic in Viv's voice.

I crawled over the seat, into the back, next to Viv. After a minute of struggling I managed to get her seatbelt unbuckled. The water was rising. I began to panic.

"Whaaa...what's...going on?" Trent had regained consciousness.

The water was up to his knees in the seat by then and he began to flail around in his seat.

"Get me out of here!"

Trent popped off his seatbelt and opened his door. Water poured in all around us.

"Georgie!" Viv grabbed tightly around my neck.

I struggled to free myself. "Viv, let me go. I'll help you get out."

Trent lumbered out of the car and landed in the lake. I could hear him hollering and splashing around from outside the car. There was nothing I could do to help him. I needed to help my sister. Trent was on his own. Besides, with his size, he would likely end up drowning us both.

I climbed outside the back driver's side window. The shocking cold water made me tense up momentarily. But the car was sinking and I needed to get my sister out, quickly. I reached in, grabbed her arm and pulled her through. The two of us swam to shore. It was only a few feet.

Crawling onto the shoreline of Red Lake, we both collapsed with exhaustion. We were soaking wet, freezing, and trying to catch our breath.

"We need to get out of here before we freeze to death," Viv exclaimed. She started climbing to her feet.

We both turned toward the water when we heard Trent yelling from somewhere out in the storm. Out in the freezing waters of Red Lake.

"We need to do something," I told my sister, standing up and moving toward the water.

Viv grabbed my arm. "Georgie, there is nothing we can do. It would be suicide for us to go out in the lake and try to bring him back in. You know that." She looked toward the road. "Let's go see if we can find help."

I agreed. We clamored up the side of the hill, to the road.

"Georgie, my leg."

We both looked down at her bandaged leg. She was beginning to bleed badly. We needed to get to the hospital right away.

"Come on, let's start walking." I knew we were only a mile or two from the hospital. We could make it. It might take a while, as Viv was limping by then.

About a quarter mile into our walk, a car screeched to a stop behind us. We both turned at the same time, as someone climbed out.

"Georgie! Is that you?" the woman called.

I couldn't see her through the gloom of the night and the raging storm all around us. But I didn't need to see her. I recognized her voice immediately. It was Ivy. I don't know how she found us, but she did. It was all I could do to hold in my relief. A flood of tears threaten to escape.

"Yes, yes it's us! Ivy!" I yelled back.

"Come on, get in the car!" She ran toward us and we both took an arm, helping Viv to hobble back to the car.

Viv and I crawled into the front seat together. Ivy had the car's heater on full blast. We were so thankful for that. I looked around at the interior.

"Whose car is this?" I asked her.

"It's my neighbor's. I hadn't heard from you, so I started to worry. I even called the hospital and there was no one there fitting your descriptions," Ivy explained. "I knew I had to come looking for you."

"Well I'm glad you did," I answered back. "Oh, about your car..."

Her hand shot up into the space between us. "No need. I saw it in the lake. I don't care about that car. I'm just glad you two are okay."

I nodded. "Hurry, please. Viv is bleeding badly."

Ivy looked down at Viv's leg, and back up into Viv's pale face. "Okay, girls, hang on!"

Three minutes later we screeched into the parking lot of the hospital's emergency room. Ivy didn't bother turning off the engine. She barely got it into park before she flew out of the car and ran into the hospital, screaming and waving her arms around like a mad woman. If the situation weren't so dire, I would have laughed at the sight.

One minute later, Viv was being wheeled on a gurney into the back, somewhere behind closed doors. Ivy and I were told, in no uncertain terms, to stay in the waiting area. I argued, to no avail. We weren't going in and that was all there was to it.

Someone did come out with a couple of heated blankets for us. We were ever so grateful for that. Ivy and I took a couple of seats in the corner of the waiting room. There was a smattering of people waiting for their loved ones to be checked out. More people than I thought there would be in a storm like this. But I guess when mother nature throws her wrath at us, there are more injuries than I would care to know about.

"Oh no!" I flew out of my chair almost as soon as I sat down. "Trent. I forgot about Trent!"

"What do you mean? Where is Trent?" Ivy asked, not sure why I was worried about him.

"He was in the car with us. Viv stabbed him in the back. Last time we saw him, he was in the lake," I tried to explain.

But there was only one part of that entire exchange that Ivy heard. "Viv stabbed him in the back?! Are you serious?"

"Yeah, he attacked me, was choking me actually, and she did what she had to do to stop him. I need to tell someone that he's out there." I headed for the nurse's desk.

I explained everything to the plump, gray haired nurse, sitting behind the desk. She listened to me with no emotion whatsoever on her face. When I was done, she finally spoke. "Let me go get my supervisor." With that, she disappeared behind a swinging brown door with a tall vertical window cut out of it.

When she returned, after what seemed like an eternity, a tall, balding man, with a salt and pepper beard, was in tow.

"Hello," he address to me. "Are you the one that drove the car into Red Lake?"

"Yes, someone needs to go get the man who was with us. I think he's still in the water."

"No, he's here," the man told me.

"He is? How?"

"Someone saw the car in the lake and called it in. The ambulance just arrived with him."

"Oh." I wondered why that person didn't stop to help if they saw the car in the water. But perhaps we had already left by then.

"Is he...is he..." I couldn't form the words to ask.

"Alive?" the man finished my sentence for me. "Yes, he's alive. Barely. He's..." he hesitated. "Are you family?"

"Um, yes, I'm his niece." I cringed at that one. But I was pretty sure it was the only way I was going to get any information on his condition. Hospitals tended to be pretty strict about that stuff.

The man looked at me from head to toe. It wasn't a creepy sort a of look, but more of a 'I don't really believe you, but I'll go along with you anyway,' sort of look. "Fine. Your uncle," he said it with emphasis, "was not breathing when the medics pulled him from the lake. But, he is breathing now. He's not conscious yet. We'll know more once he wakes up. Stay out here in the waiting room and I'll have someone come get you when he wakes."

With that, the man turned and disappeared behind that same brown swinging door.

I walked back over and told Ivy everything I had learned.

"It's time we got the sheriff involved, don't you think?" Ivy asked me.

I nodded.

Beverly finally arrived. Soggy and frantic. She ran to me and could barely speak. It looked like she had run the entire way over.

"I was finally able to get someone to bring me over. She dropped me off." Beverly grabbed onto my arm. "Is Viv okay?"

"Yeah, I think so. She's been back there for a while. No one has told us anything," I explained.

She set her jaw in a determined manner and turned toward the nurse's desk. "Well, that's about to change."

After a short conversation with the nurse on duty, Beverly went right into the exam room where Viv was being looked after. The two of them returned a half hour later. Viv was all bandaged up and was looking more like herself. Save for her disheveled appearance from being out in the storm.

I introduced Beverly and Ivy. Neither seemed surprised, or even bothered, by the other. They were both mothers. They were both my mother, and I loved them both. They could see that.

Ivy drove all of us home. Once Beverly put Viv to bed, she came back downstairs and made tea for the three of us. My two mothers and I sat down at the kitchen table to talk.

Ivy and I told Beverly everything. We left nothing out. My kidnapping, Trent's part in it, Stan's part in it, all of it. We even told her about how Ivy and I kept reliving our lives. I explained that Trent was responsible for me dying multiple times. Of course, the reliving our lives thing stunned her most of all. But she believed us. I loved her more than I ever had at that moment.

The next morning, all of us, including Viv, made a visit to the sheriff's office. We told them everything. Well almost everything. We left out the reliving our lives part.

Before Trent was released from the hospital, he was arrested. The handcuffs held him nicely to the metal frame of the bed.

Of course, Trent denied it all. I wouldn't expect anything less. But Ivy, Beverly, Viv, and myself were enough to convince the sheriff that it all happened.

Stan confessed to knowing about the kidnapping, but he insisted that he found out afterward. He just chose not to tell anyone. Not even his wife. He will have to pay for that for a while, but I still love him. That won't change.

Though I'm an adult, I took Ivy up on her offer and moved in with her. Beverly was probably a bit hurt by that, but she understood. I needed to get to know my first mother better.

Harper and Jack have unofficially adopted Viv as their new sister also. We all hang out often.

Now that I'm no longer in danger from Trent and his goons, I'm curious as to what this life will bring.

The End

～

Have you read the Stone Mountain Family Saga yet?

WINTERS LEGEND ON STONE MOUNTAIN

Some families will do whatever it takes to win.

Carson Winters does as he pleases, without guilt or shame. And no one can stop him. But his judgment day is coming.

This series about the Winters family is a complicated tale of the family with everything. You won't want to miss a single word of this story of love, loss, and heartache, with just a bit of mayhem thrown in.

The complete Stone Mountain Family Saga:
Winters Legend on Stone Mountain
A Dangerous Game on Stone Mountain
Deceit on Stone Mountain

～

If you enjoyed this book and would like information on new releases, sign up for my newsletter here:

www.MichelleFiles.com
Thank you!

CPSIA information can be obtained
at www.ICGtesting.com
Printed in the USA
BVHW091134150621
609530BV00011B/1946